1/6/18

This book should be returned/renewed by the latest date shown above. Overdue items incur charges which prevent self-service renewals. Please contact the library.

Wandsworth Libraries
24 hour Renewal Hotline
01159 293388
www.wandsworth.gov.uk

Wandsworth

About the Author

Ross Montgomery started writing stories as a teenager, when he really should have been doing homework, and continued doing so at university. After graduating, he experimented with working as a pig farmer and a postman before deciding to channel these skills into teaching at a primary school. He wrote his debut *Alex, the Dog and the Unopenable Door* when he really should have been marking homework. It was shortlisted for the Costa Book Award and nominated for the 2014 Branford Boase Award. *The Tornado Chasers* is his second book. He lives in Brixton, London, with his girlfriend, a cat and many, many dead plants.

The Tornado Chasers

Ross Montgomery

FABER & FABER

First published in 2014
by Faber and Faber Limited
Bloomsbury House,
74–77 Great Russell Street,
London, WC1B 3DA

Typeset by Crow Books
Printed in England by CPI Group (UK) Ltd, Croydon, CR0 4YY

A CIP record for this book
is available from the British Library

ISBN 978–0–571–29842–6

To Helen –
for everything,
obviously

Dear Warden,

If you're reading this letter then it means I've finally escaped.

It also means you've found the secret place behind the loose tile above the sink, which means you'll have also found the mouse traps I put there before I left. ~~Sorry about~~ Actually I'm not sorry about that.

When I first came to the County Detention Centre, they said I had to tell the truth about what happened - when it all began, who did what, why we did it, why

1

it ended the way it did. 'Write it down,'
they said. 'Make a poem about it all. Turn
it into a story if you have to. But one
way or another, you have to tell us.'

And so I did. I sat down, and I wrote
a story - about everything that happened,
from the beginning to the end, as best as
I could tell it. The only way I could tell
it. And here it is - every last word.

Which brings me to the question I know
you're desperate to ask: if I've run
away, then where have I run away <u>to</u>?

Well, you're just going to have to read my
story, aren't you?

~~LOVE~~ YOURS SINCERELY,

INMATE 409

1

How It Began

MY NAME IS OWEN UNDERWOOD,
I AM 11 YEARS OLD TODAY,
AND THIS IS THE WORST BIRTHDAY
OF MY LIFE.

The last sentence I wrote in my diary, before it all happened.

To be fair it was the *only* sentence I wrote in my diary. The other pages I just left blank, and they stayed that way right up until the police searched my room weeks later and stamped the word 'EVIDENCE' on the front in red ink. I didn't have time to write down anything else, of course, because of everything that happened that night.

I was lying under my bed, which was wrapped with chicken wire and surrounded by several dozen sandbags. This was in case the tornado ripped the roof off the house, or threw a boulder through the wall, or a ravenous bear broke the shutters and tried to climb through the window – which is why my parents had also given me a can of bear repellent. I hadn't used it yet, which was a relief because it had a label on the side that said the spray made you go blind if you inhaled it.

You might be wondering why I had a can of bear repellent, or why my bed was wrapped in chicken wire and sandbags. Maybe you don't live in a village like Barrow. Consider yourself lucky. When my parents told me just a few weeks before that we were moving to Barrow because of the tornado warning, I was pretty confused. No one in Skirting had ever seemed bothered about the storms. There hadn't been one in the valleys for over ten years. If we moved, I'd have to leave all my friends behind, and my school, right before the summer holidays. Mum and Dad said they had no choice – Barrow was the only safe place left to live in the valleys. And that made me even *more* confused.

What was there to be afraid of in the valleys?

And that was when they told me about the bear attacks.

'OWEN!'

The shout came from behind my bedroom door. I

startled, and smacked my head on the underside of the bed. Luckily I was wearing my crash helmet.

(I probably should have mentioned this earlier.)

I suffer from something called startling. Every time something happens that I don't expect – like a loud noise or a sudden movement – I lose control of my body for a bit. I've had it all my life. It's why I have to wear a helmet all the time. Luckily people are very understanding about it. At least, they were before I moved to Barrow.

I clambered out from under the bed, shaking the twitch out of my neck.

'Y-yes, Dad?'

'Your dinner's ready,' came his voice from the other side of the door.

I glanced around my bedroom. There wasn't much to look at. No toys, books, posters – nothing. All that was left was the bed, a single bare light bulb hanging from the ceiling, and the closed wooden shutters over the windows. Even my bedroom door handle was padded with foam. I walked over to the door and gave it a wiggle. It didn't move. Which wasn't surprising, given that my parents had just locked me inside.

(I probably should have mentioned *that* earlier, too.)

'Everything OK in there, darling?' came another

voice from behind the door. 'Having a nice birthday?'

'Yes, Mum,' I lied. 'It's wonderful.'

'Well, we've got a treat for you!' said Dad excitedly. 'Are you wearing your helmet?'

I gave it a loud knock with my fist. 'Yes, Dad.'

'Good boy,' said Mum. 'Now, stand back! It's very hot.'

I took several steps back.

'Here we go!' said Dad.

A ham and pineapple pizza slowly emerged from under the crack of the doorway. The ham had been arranged into a number '11'. It was quickly followed by a pair of yellow rubber gloves.

'Put the gloves on before you touch it,' said Dad sternly. 'In case of burns. Obviously we can't give you a knife or a fork because you might accidentally cut your fingers off and die.'

'And don't forget his cake!' added Mum.

'Oh yes,' said Dad. 'I almost forgot.'

A single pop-tart slid out from under the door and came to a stop by my feet.

'Happy 11th Birthday Owen!' said my parents in unison.

I sighed. Time for another lie.

'Wow. Thanks, Mum and Dad,' I said. 'What a treat.'

'Well, it *is* a special day,' said Dad. 'Anything else you need, Owen?'

I swallowed. Time for the truth – finally.

'Er . . . there is, actually,' I said. 'Dad, Mum – can I ask a favour?'

'Of course you can!' said Dad.

'You can ask us anything,' said Mum.

'Good,' I said, 'Well, I was wondering if maybe you could maybe, you know . . . let me out of my room for a bit?'

There was a stony silence on the other side of the door.

'You know we can't do that, Owen,' said Dad. 'It's far too dangerous. There's a raging tornado outside Barrow as we speak.'

'Besides, darling, don't forget about all those *bears* outside,' Mum added. 'Just because there's a tornado it doesn't mean they stop hunting the valleys for food. They could be outside your window right now.'

I glanced at the shutters behind me. They creaked menacingly in the wind. I gulped.

'I . . . I suppose,' I said.

'Glad you agree.' Mum sighed with relief. 'Anything *else* we can get our little birthday boy?'

I looked down at the pizza and the pop-tart. 'Maybe a drink?'

'Of course!' said Dad.

A plate of water slid out from under the doorway.

'Thanks,' I said dejectedly.

'Eat it quickly, darling!' said Mum. 'Remember the rules of the curfew – lights off at 6 p.m.'

My heart sank the moment she said it.

Six o'clock already! But then that meant . . .

'Ten minutes!' said Mum. 'And then straight to bed. Night, sweetie!'

I listened to their footsteps fade down the corridor in despair. This really was the worst birthday of my life. Not only was I locked inside my bedroom, with no friends or presents, but I only had ten minutes left until six o'clock.

The plan was going to go ahead without me.

I stared forlornly at my birthday dinner on the floor. Two miserable plates and a pop-tart. I didn't even have enough hands to carry them to my bed at the same time. I could have held the pop-tart in my mouth, of course – but knowing Mum and Dad, they'd tell me that I shouldn't, in case I suddenly startled and I choked on it and died . . .

A rebellious grin spread across my face.

Go on, Owen. They'll never know.

I pressed my ear to the door to make sure Mum and

Dad were nowhere near. Then I carefully placed the pop-tart between my teeth, picked up the plates, and swaggered to the bed with all three together.

'The perfect crime,' I mumbled.

Tap tap.

I startled.

You know what that means by now. First, my whole body seized up. My teeth clenched shut, and I bit straight through the pop-tart. One hand threw the plateful of water all over my face, and the other flung the pizza across the other side of the room where it stuck to the wall with a meaty *splat*.

'Who's there?' I cried, swinging round.

No one answered. My room was, of course, empty. It wasn't as if there were many places where someone could hide, either. I looked down at the remains of my birthday pop-tart, which had shattered into flavourless crumbs on the floor.

'Great,' I muttered. 'Well, that's just . . .'

Tap tap.

I startled again, ever so slightly. This time I knew exactly where the sound was coming from. My eyes flew to the closed wooden shutters.

There was something outside the window.

'H-hello?' I said nervously.

There was no response. I stood, frozen to the spot, water dripping off my hair. All I could hear were the storm reports on the radio downstairs and the rush of the wind on the shutters and the quickening *tap, tap, tap* of my heart. Behind me the pizza slowly slid down the wall, leaving the number '11' perfectly spelled out in ham on the wallpaper.

I gulped. 'Mum? Dad . . . ?'

And then all of a sudden it came again, louder, harder, the shutters trembling on their hinges with each strike. *THUMP. THUMP.*

There was no doubt about it. It was a bear attack. Within seconds I was back behind the sandbags around my bed, wielding the can of bear repellent towards the shutters with trembling hands.

'D-don't come any closer!' I cried. 'This is highly flammable, and should never be used in an unventilated room—'

I was cut off by a loud groan from the other side of the shutters.

'Owen, you pillock,' said a voice. 'It's the *secret knock*. Remember?'

I recognised the voice immediately. It almost made me startle again.

'*You?*' I said.

'It's the whole point of the secret knock,' the voice continued angrily. 'I knock twice so you know it's me, and then you let me in. Christ! I've only explained it to you about a *thousand* times.' There was a loud sigh. 'Look – just let me in.'

I fumbled.

'I . . . I can't,' I said. 'The shutters are locked from the outside. My parents decided to . . .'

'Oh, forget it!' the voice muttered furiously. 'I'll just do it myself.'

A plastic ruler slid between the shutters and wiggled up, lifting the clasp that held the two panels together. They flew open, and at once the room was swept with a bracing wind that sent leaves swirling in great gusts across the floor.

Standing on my windowsill, a ruler in one hand and a samurai sword in the other, was Callum Brenner. At least, I was pretty certain it was him. It was hard to tell because he was wearing a balaclava.

'Such a *pillock*,' he muttered, throwing the ruler at me.

I smiled. It was definitely Callum Brenner. He leapt off the windowsill.

'Well, what are you waiting for?' he snapped. 'It's almost six! We're supposed to be at the meeting!'

My eyes bugged. 'You mean . . .'

Callum rolled his eyes. 'Yes, wussbag, *the meeting*! Tonight's the night – remember? The night it all happens! Everything we've been planning! You. Me.' He struck a dramatic pose. '*The Tornado Chasers*.'

That was how it began, in one respect. How I was able to escape my bedroom, and leave the village, and go chasing a huge tornado across the valleys. But it doesn't explain the whole story. It doesn't say *why* we decided to do it in the first place – risk our lives, break the law, do the unthinkable. And most times, the *why* is much more important than the *how*. I know that now.

So I'm going to go back to the day it *really* began – a week earlier, my very first day in Barrow.

The first day I met Callum Brenner.

2

The First Day I Met Callum Brenner

'Hold still, Owen!'

'Come over here so I can tie your shoelaces.'

'Stop moving!'

'If your shoelaces aren't tied up you might trip over them or get them stuck in heavy machinery and rip your legs off.'

I stood in the empty playground of Barrow Prep, my parents barking orders either side of me and pulling at my arms like two dogs with a piece of rope. I felt sick and nervous, and not just because it was my first day at my new school. We had only just moved to Barrow the day before – I didn't know *anyone* yet. I had no idea what my new teacher would be like, or whether I'd make any new friends. To make it worse, none of them would know about my crash helmet. I'd have to explain about my condition to the whole class. I stepped away from my parents, smiling sheepishly.

'Er . . . I should probably get inside now, Mum and Dad,' I said. 'I don't want to be late on my very first day! I'm sure I look fine.'

In fact I didn't look fine, I looked like a total idiot, but that wasn't really my fault. My new school uniform was bright yellow from top to bottom, including the shorts. Mum leant down and smeared a spitty thumb across my cheek.

'You're sure you're OK, poppum?' she said. 'You don't want us to come in and tell all your new friends about your condition?'

I balked. 'No! I mean – no thank you, Mum.'

She sighed. 'Just remember, all the valleys are under Storm Warning 5 now. We haven't had an SW5 for ten years! And don't forget, SW5 means . . .'

'. . . A tornado could touch down any time without warning,' I said mechanically. 'I'll be safe, Mum, I promise.'

'You'd *better* be safe, Owen,' said Dad sternly. 'An SW5 is no laughing matter. You were too young to remember the last one. The tornado could arrive *tomorrow* for all we know! At least here in Barrow people understand how serious that is. Look – see how many stormtraps they have here!'

He pointed behind me, to the hills that surrounded the entire village. Along the top ran an unbroken ring of red lights, wrapping round the valley like a net. It certainly looked impressive. Back in Skirting, we'd only had one stormtrap to protect the entire village, stuck on top of the church. Barrow must have had hundreds.

'People in Barrow value safety above everything else,' Dad explained. 'That's why they have a curfew for children every day at 4 p.m., so there's no chance of anyone wandering around outside too late. And being eaten by the bears.'

'That's right!' said Mum. 'So no dawdling or chatting with your new friends after school – come straight home.' Her face suddenly hardened to stone. 'And for heaven's sake, Owen – *no climbing trees!*'

Dad grabbed me by the shoulders.

'We mean it, Owen!' he cried desperately. 'Not after what happened last time! Promise us, Owen!'

'Promise us!' Mum wailed, grabbing my arms.

A bell suddenly rang inside the school. I pulled free and made a grateful dash for freedom before they could try to stop me.

'I won't!' I shouted over my shoulder. 'Promise!'

My parents have always been like that – overprotective. Sometimes I think if they could wrap me in bubble wrap, they would. Actually they did once. It was the worst swimming lesson of my life.

As I stepped inside the school, the nervous grip on my chest got tighter and tighter. I was obviously late, and the corridors were empty. By the time I found the room I was looking for, my stomach was almost twisting itself into knots. I looked at the poster that covered the door in front of me.

KNOW YOUR BARROW STORM LAWS!

1. *Curfew begins at four o'clock each day!*
2. *Lights out at six o'clock!*
3. *Whenever you're outside, stick with your Home-Time Partner!*
4. *Always wear your highly visible yellow uniform so you can be seen by adults!*
5. *NEVER LEAVE BARROW UNDER ANY CIRCUMSTANCES.*
6. *Remember, if you don't want to follow the Storm Laws, there's always room for you at the COUNTY DETENTION CENTRE!*

I took a moment to calm myself, and knocked on the door.

'Come in!' a voice sang from inside.

I opened the door and peeked inside. Thirty children sat in tight rows, all wearing the same bright yellow uniform, looking directly at me. They were all holding scripts. I had obviously interrupted them. There was no sign of a teacher. I looked back at the rows of silent children.

'Excuse me,' I said, stepping inside. 'Is this Miss Pewlish's cla—?'

'*RAAAAAARGH!*'

A giant bear suddenly leapt out at me from behind the door, its eyes bugging wildly out of its head as it waved a set of razor-sharp claws. I screamed and flung myself sideways into a stack of books, sending them crashing down on top of me. I glanced up in terror, expecting to see a ravenous bear standing over me. Instead I saw a woman in her thirties. She was wearing a pair of giant fake bear paws on her hands, and held a fake bear head under her arm. She glared at me disapprovingly.

'Abysmal,' she said. 'If I've said it once, I've said it a thousand times: *never enter a room without checking the vital points*. Bears love nothing more than hiding behind a closed door, waiting for a *careless* child to wander inside.' She turned to the class. 'Who else can name me some vital points?'

The children's hands shot up.

'Wardrobes!' said one.

'Behind sofas!' said another.

'Inside fridges and under large rugs!'

The woman nodded. 'Not bad. As for *you*,' she said, pointing at me with an outstretched claw, '*you* should know better. Walking into a room without checking behind the door! Where do you think we are – *Skirting?* Get up this instant!'

I scrambled to free myself from under the pile of books. 'Sorry, I . . .'

'And what's this?' she said, rapping her claws against my helmet. 'Cycling to school? When a Storm Warning 5 has just been announced across the valleys? Unbelievable!'

'No, it's not . . .' I attempted.

'*Clearly*,' she boomed over me, 'this child does not have a single clue about safety, or the Storm Laws either! Do you *want* to end up in the County Detention Centre, young man? How many months have you even been in this class, er . . . whatever your name is?'

'I . . . er . . . none,' I whimpered. 'I'm Owen Underwood. I just moved here. This is my first day.'

The woman blinked. She cleared her throat.

'Ah,' she muttered awkwardly. 'Yes. Owen Underwood. Of course.'

She quickly removed the giant paws and dropped them onto her desk.

'Welcome, Owen,' she said brightly, as if nothing had happened. 'I'm Miss Pewlish, your new class teacher and School Safety Officer. You're very lucky to join us for these last few weeks before the holidays – we're due to perform a play for Barrow history day!'

Miss Pewlish shoved a script into my hands and wheeled me towards the rest of the class, who were still staring at me.

'Don't be shy!' she bellowed. 'Introduce yourself!'

I looked at the rows of children in front of me. My throat dried.

'Er . . . hello,' I said. 'My name is Owen Underwood. My parents and I just moved here yesterday, after the valleys went under SW5. They figured where we were living wasn't safe enough any more.' I gulped. 'We're originally from, er . . . Skirting, actually.'

I knew immediately that I shouldn't have said it. There was a dark mutter across the class. The children glanced at each other.

'*Skirting*,' said Miss Pewlish, unable to hide a note of

disdain in her voice. 'Well, no wonder you don't know a thing about the Storm Laws! How nice to have a child from somewhere so, er . . . *different*.'

She glanced at the top of my head. She tried to think of a delicate way to word her question, and then gave up entirely.

'And why are you wearing a crash helmet, Owen?'

Some of the children giggled. I sighed. Might as well get it over with. I turned back to the thirty faces staring at me.

'Thank you for asking, Miss Pewlish,' I said. 'I suffer from what's known as a *Delayed Startle Reflex*. It means that if I get surprised, I lose control of my body for a second or two. Most children have a startle reflex when they're babies, although they lose it some time when they're between six to twelve months old. It is quite rare to be found in someone my age. While I *do* have to wear my helmet for my own protection, I am nevertheless able to lead a perfectly normal life with my condition. And don't worry, it's not contagious. Ha ha.'

No one laughed.

'How interesting,' said Miss Pewlish, not sounding in the least bit interested. 'Well, Owen, let's get you sorted with a Home-Time Partner right away so you can shut up and we can all stop looking at you.'

I blinked. 'Er . . . Home-Time Partner?'

Miss Pewlish rolled her eyes. 'Yes, *Home-Time Partner*! I'm sure they have no need for them in somewhere as carefree and riotous as Skirting!'

She rummaged through her desk drawers and emerged with a single sheet of paper.

'In Barrow, children walk between school and home each day with a partner. It means they're less likely to be late for curfew and be savaged by bears. You'll be too old for one *next* year, of course – but you'll need one for these last few weeks. Better safe than sorry!'

She glanced over the list of names.

'We'll pair you up with your closest neighbour,' she muttered. 'Can you remember which street you live on?'

'Um . . . Magnolia Crescent, I think,' I said nervously.

There was an audible gasp across the room. The children in front of me covered their mouths and snorted with delight.

'Not *Callum*!'

'I can't believe it!'

'He won't last a *week*!'

Miss Pewlish found the name on the list. Any softness in her face immediately disappeared. She clenched her jaw.

'*Callum . . . Brenner*,' she said, each word an accusation.

The tables before me immediately parted, leaving a clear path to the back of the classroom. There, sat alone, was a boy. He was slightly too big for his chair, and was making up for it by leaning it back and balancing it on one leg. His desk was covered in broken pencils. All the other desks around him were empty, and scattered with screwed-up balls of paper. He looked me up and down in disgust.

'Are you *serious*?' he said. 'I'm not walking home . . . with *that*!'

Miss Pewlish's left eyelid started twitching uncontrollably, like a fly in a web.

'*Tough!*' she shouted. 'You'll do as you're told, Callum Brenner! You've been walking home with the Cartwright twins for long enough – I think it's time we finally gave them a break.'

She indicated a boy and a girl in the front row, who were wiping tears of gratitude from their eyes and mouthing the words 'thank you' at the ceiling.

Callum kicked the desk. 'But *Victoria* . . . '

'Stop calling me that!' Miss Pewlish snapped, her cheeks trembling. 'One more peep out of you, Callum Brenner, and I'll have you repeating the entire year *again*!'

The class sniggered. Callum shot them a hateful look,

22

and fell silent, his hand tightly gripping a pencil beside him. Miss Pewlish nudged me forwards.

'Go on then, Owen,' she muttered. 'Go and, er . . . sit next to him.'

I slowly made my way through the pathway of tables towards Callum. The other children could barely hide their delight at my suffering, like I'd been caught painting swear words on a fence by my mum or I'd just dropped my ice cream down the toilet. Not one of them said hello to me, or waved, or even tried to be friendly. Miss Pewlish was right – Barrow wasn't like Skirting at all.

I sat down on the back row and glanced at my new partner. Callum stared back at me, his mouth open in disgust. I swallowed nervously. I'd never had any trouble making friends back in Skirting. All I had to do was be myself, and ask lots of questions. I nodded to the screwed-up pieces of paper on the floor.

'Wow,' I said. 'Look at all that paper! You must really like writing.'

Callum gripped his pencil tighter. I cleared my throat.

'So,' I said. 'I guess we're partners now.'

I held out my hand, and put on my best cowboy voice.

'Put it there, partner,' I said.

Callum snapped his pencil in two.

3

The Hardest Boy
in Barrow

The read-through for the play lasted all morning. Then
after lunch, we did it all over again. Neither Callum nor
I had any lines, so we sat in silence and followed the
words in the script. At least, *I* followed them. Callum
ripped out the pages and threw them at people.

Finally the bell rang for the end of the day. Miss
Pewlish immediately dropped her script and leapt to
the door, waving a rattle above her head.

'Quarter to four!' she cried. 'Fifteen minutes to get
home before curfew starts! Go, go, go!'

The children flew from their desks without another
word, grabbing their partners and racing out the
classroom.

'GO! GO! GO!' Miss Pewlish bellowed after the evacuating children. 'And don't forget, the day after tomorrow is Presentation Day! Make sure you all have something prepared!'

I quickly got to my feet and looked around for my partner. Callum was grabbing pots of pencils from off the windowsill and emptying them into his bag. I took his hand. He swung round in horror and shoved me backwards.

'What are you doing?' he yelled.

I startled. 'I-I thought I was supposed to hold your hand.'

'No!' said Callum. 'No, you're not!'

'Oh,' I muttered. 'Er . . . sorry.'

Callum wiped his hand on his trousers and stormed out the classroom. I watched him leave in despair.

'Hey! Partner! Wait for me!'

'He'll wait outside,' said a voice behind me. 'He always does.'

I spun round. At the nearest desk, a girl was slowly packing up her bag. She had more hair than anyone I had ever seen in my life, and it was sticking out in all directions. She had even tried to hold it in place with a hairband, and had failed. Stood beside her was a boy. He was huge – a foot taller than me at least, maybe twice

my width. He gazed down at me, calmly and blankly –
like a horse. I gulped.

'Er . . . I beg your pardon?' I said.

The girl didn't turn to look at me, or smile when she
talked.

'He can't walk home without a partner. Not unless he
wants to get in trouble.' She zipped up her bag. 'Just try
to stay on his good side. Not that he has one.'

'Oh. Thanks,' I said.

I turned to get my bag from the table, and paused.
Perhaps this was the time to make some friends. I
quickly finished packing my bag and turned around, my
hand held out.

'I'm sorry, I didn't get either of your names . . .'

But I was alone. The girl and the boy had both left
the classroom without saying another word.

Outside, the playground was empty. In the distance I
could see the other children sprinting across the village
green. Just like the girl said, Callum was waiting for me
at the bottom of the steps. He scowled up at me.

'Hurry up.'

I scurried after him as he strode out of the playground
and past the clock tower, crossing over the bridge and
turning onto the path that ran beside the stream. I
turned around to glance at the clock tower before it

disappeared from sight. A stormtrap jutted out the top like a set of traffic lights. The red light on the front blinked away the seconds until curfew started.

We walked in silence, the ferns buzzing in the summer air beside us. It was hard to believe that a tornado could touch down in the valleys at any moment. It seemed so calm.

'So,' I said cheerfully, trying to make conversation. 'Are you looking forward to the class play?'

'No,' said Callum. 'It's stupid.'

'Oh,' I said.

We kept walking.

'What about . . . Presentation Day?' I tried. 'Is that . . . also stupid?'

Callum nodded. 'Yeah. Everyone has to do a presentation, in front of the whole class.'

'Oh, I see,' I said, nodding. 'That's very interesting. What are you going to do yours on?'

'I'm not going to do one,' said Callum bluntly.

I looked at him with confusion. 'Isn't it for homework?'

He stopped, and glared at me.

'Of course it's for homework,' he snapped. 'That's why I'm not going to do it.'

He looked at me for a while, as if he was weighing me up. Finally he sighed, and folded his arms.

'Look,' he said. 'Let's get this sorted. From now on, you can't look like you're with me. If anyone comes near us, you hide in the bushes. Got it?'

I looked at the 'bushes' beside the path. They were big patches of stinging nettles. Callum grabbed me by the shoulder and leant in.

'Let me explain,' he said. 'I'm kind of a big deal round here. Truth is, I'm the hardest kid in Barrow. So I can't be seen walking around with a dweebus like you – everyone would lose respect for me, wouldn't they?'

I frowned. '*Dweebus?* What do you mean, dwee—'

'Glad you understand,' said Callum, patting me on the back. He glanced round nervously. 'Now let's get out of here quickly, before . . .'

'Well well well,' said a voice behind us. 'Look who it is!'

Callum's face visibly drained of colour. I turned around. Three boys were standing on the path behind us. Instead of school uniform they wore neon yellow tracksuits, strapped at the elbows and knees with pads and high-visibility strips. Each of their sweaters was emblazoned with the words JUNIOR SAFETY WARDEN. A boy at the front stepped forwards, swinging a shiny whistle on a chain.

'Well, boys,' he said, tutting loudly. 'Looks like we've

found two stragglers who think they don't have to hurry home during an SW5!' He fixed Callum with a mocking expression. 'Honestly, Callum Brenner. At *your* age you should know better.'

The other two boys snickered, nudging the boy in front. Callum attempted to regain his composure.

'Oh, hi guys!' he said. 'Just, er . . . doing the daily rounds, are you?'

'Yep,' said the boy at the front, adjusting his elbow pads with an air of importance. 'Checking the streets are clear, making the village a safer place for everyone . . . no big deal. How about you – still playing with crayons in Miss Pewlish's class?'

The boys either side of him collapsed into snorting laughter. The front boy nodded his approval, and then turned to look at me.

'And, er . . . who's this?'

Callum's eyes filled with dread. The other boys stepped forwards.

'You must be new,' said one. 'You don't look like you're from round here.'

'Nice helmet,' said the other.

I smiled. 'Thank you! It's for my condition. You see, I suffer from what's known as a *Delayed Startle Reflex*. It means that I have a dramatic and involuntary response . . .'

Beside me, Callum was struggling to calm his breathing. The boy in front looked from me to Callum, and then back to me again. His face lit up.

'Hang on a second,' he said. 'This isn't your . . . *Home-Time Partner*, is it Callum?'

Callum flushed a furious red. 'N-no! He's not!'

'*Really*,' said the boy. 'So the two of you are walking home together . . . why, exactly?'

Callum floundered. 'I . . . er . . . he . . .'

'I can answer that one,' I said helpfully.

I pushed Callum aside, who stood open-mouthed with what I could only assume was gratitude.

'Don't worry,' I said. 'Callum's already explained to me about how well-respected he is around here. He only needs a Home-Time Partner for a few more weeks, and then he can go back to being the hardest boy in Barrow.' I turned to him with a helpful smile. 'Isn't that right, Callum?'

For a moment, the boys stared at me in disbelief. Then they burst out laughing.

'Oh *wow*!' said the one in front. 'The hardest boy in Barrow? That's priceless!'

'What else did you tell him, Callum?' said one of the other boys. 'That you're a superhero? That you can travel through time?'

Callum was utterly humiliated. He stood, ashen-faced, his eyes welling up. In front of him the boys laughed harder and harder, leaning on each other for support. I stepped forward.

'Er – Callum,' I said, tugging on his sleeve. 'Maybe we should just go . . .'

Callum snapped. In one movement he had lifted me straight off the ground by my jumper. I struggled.

'Wait – what are you doing?' I cried. 'Put me down!'

'*Shut up!*' he cried, his face screwed tight with furious tears. 'You don't tell me what to do, you . . . you *wimp*! Nobody does! Just stay away and *leave me alone*!'

With that, he swung round and threw me head first into a pile of stinging nettles. There was a moment of calm before my skin suddenly came alive, the pain singing across my hands and face and bare legs. I flew to my feet, my whole body burning bright with pain. Callum was storming off down the pathway in the distance. The three Junior Wardens waved him off, laughing hysterically.

'Hey! Super Callum!' they cried. 'Come back! You left your sidekick behind!'

4

Ceri, Orlaith and Murderous Pete

[Enter VILLAGERS in torn and ragged peasant clothing, looking woeful.]

VILLAGER 1: Hark! Have you heard the news, fellow
   villagers? Another tornado hath landed in the valleys!
VILLAGER 2: Zounds! Not again!
VILLAGER 3: How long doth we have to wait until
   someone finally maketh a tornado-proof village?
VILLAGER 1: [in horror] Gadzooks! Here it comes now!

[With great dramatic flourish and extremely loud crashing of
cymbals, enter TORNADO. At the back of the stage a single
BUSH startles and leaps into the air, getting tangled up in the

fairy lights that are supposed to represent the starry night sky.]

BUSH: Ah, oops. Sorry. Ouch.
TORNADO: [*exasperated*] Again?
BUSH: [*twitching*] Sorry. Er . . . can somebody help me
   out please?

I struggled hopelessly in the wires as the rest of the
cast snickered quietly around me. From offstage, I could
hear Miss Pewlish sigh with frustration.

'Owen,' she said. 'This isn't going to work.'

I looked up. Miss Pewlish was sat on a deckchair in
the middle of the school hall, wearing a bright yellow
beret with a badge on the front saying 'WRITER/
DIRECTOR' that she had obviously made herself.

'Sorry, Miss Pewlish,' I said. 'I startled.'

'Yes, Owen, I can see that,' she said. 'But unfortunately,
bushes aren't meant to startle. They're supposed to
stand still, or rustle menacingly if need be.' She sighed.
'Why don't you just . . . stick with Callum for now?'

I nodded, my face burning, and scurried offstage to a
chorus of sniggers. My face was of course burning both
from embarrassment and the remains of the stinging
nettles from the day before. I sat down on a bench at
the back of the hall and tried to hide from everyone.

'That was brilliant,' said a familiar voice behind me. 'Martin Price jumps out wearing a glittery sequined leotard, and you almost wet yourself. Is there anything you're *not* frightened of?'

I turned around angrily. Callum was leaning back on a plastic chair behind me, ripping up his script. Despite attacking me he had still turned up at my front door that morning and walked with me to school, as if nothing had happened.

'I wasn't frightened,' I said. 'I startled. It's my condition.'

Callum snorted. 'You looked pretty frightened to me.'

I almost answered back, but quickly held my tongue. I had been almost a whole minute late home for curfew after yesterday's incident. My parents took one look at my stinging nettle burns and scabbed knees, and had accused me of trying to climb trees. They had sent me straight to bed. I didn't argue with them – I was too upset and humiliated to tell the truth. But I wasn't going to let it happen again.

'Well . . . whatever,' I mumbled sheepishly.

'Right,' cried Miss Pewlish at the front of the stage, 'let's try again, shall we?'

[*With great dramatic flourish and extremely loud crashing of cymbals, enter TORNADO.*]

TORNADO: Behold! I am the tornado, the greatest of all natural disasters. You are powerless against me!

[Enter THOMAS BARROW to triumphant music.]

THOMAS BARROW: That's where you're wrong, Tornado!

VILLAGER 1: Egad! 'Tis Thomas Barrow, local genius.

THOMAS BARROW: Villagers! We careful and cautious types have lived in danger for too long. To that I say – no more!

VILLAGERS: [*all together*] Hear! Hear!

THOMAS BARROW: That's why I've decided to make a new village – one safe from storms and dangers. Somewhere over there, I think. It shall be named . . . BARROW. Who's with me?

VILLAGERS: [*all together*] Huzzah!

[VILLAGERS carry THOMAS BARROW offstage on their shoulders, cheering.]

'Of course,' said a voice about a centimetre from my left ear, 'that's not really how it happened.'

I startled, and swung round. A girl had sat down on the bench beside me. She was wearing a hat with a piece of card in the brim that said 'PRESS', and had a massive camera around her neck.

'I beg your pardon?' I said. 'How what happened?'

'That's not how the village was made,' said the girl, pointing at the play. 'There *was* no Thomas Barrow. Miss Pewlish made him up. I looked it all up in the library. Want to know the truth? Barrow was only built about ten years ago!'

I frowned, and looked at the stage. 'But . . . why would Miss Pewlish lie about it?'

The girl sighed. 'Well, I *did* ask her that. She said never to call her house at the weekend again. Also she said she can say whatever she flipping well wants because it's her flipping play and she has an "Artistic Licence".' The girl shook her head in admiration. 'Sounds great, doesn't it? An "Artistic Licence". I have to get myself one of those.'

The girl looked jealously at the play unfolding onstage. I cleared my throat. Here it was: my first proper chance to make a friend.

'I like your costume,' I said.

The girl glanced at me. 'Hmm? What?'

'Your costume,' I said, pointing at her hat. 'Are you a reporter in the play or something?'

She frowned, confused. 'I'm not in the play.'

I paused.

'Oh,' I said.

The girl stuck out her hand. 'Ceri Dewbridge – Head Reporter for the *Dewbridge Gazette*. Miss Pewlish said I can't be in the play because I'm too much of a "liability", whatever that means. I'm doing a report on it instead.' She cackled. 'That'll show her! My damning exposé's going to blow this whole place *wide open* when I deliver it at Presentation Day tomorrow.'

My stomach dropped.

'Presentation Day,' I muttered. 'I forgot.'

'Hmm? What?' she said. 'Oh, yeah, presentations. They're really scary. You have to get up in front of the whole class and talk about something really important for two whole minutes. And it has to be good, otherwise you get a bad mark. What's yours going to be on . . . whatever-your-name-is?'

I held out my hand. 'Owen.'

Ceri's eyes suddenly widened.

'Hang on – Owen! The new boy! The one who fainted yesterday in class! I didn't recognise you, all dressed up like a bush.'

I blushed. 'I didn't faint. It was an involuntary reac—'

But Ceri had already started taking photos of me.

'Brilliant,' she said. 'I can see the headline now:

New Boy Thrown Offstage For Fainting After Hours Of Gruelling Rehearsals. It'll be the story of the month – the year, even! I might actually *sell* a newspaper!' She held up her notepad. 'Mind if I ask you a few questions for my report?'

I was about to say no, but then I realised that Ceri was the first person to be nice to me since I'd arrived. I shrugged.

'Er . . . sure,' I said. 'Ask away.'

Ceri beamed. 'Great! So, tell me, Owen: what's your role now you've been humiliatingly demoted to backstage duties?'

I blinked. 'I'm not sure. I think I'm working with Callum.'

'I don't think Callum has a job,' said Ceri.

I looked behind me. Callum was chewing his script into spitballs and throwing them at the lighting crew.

'Doesn't look like it,' I muttered.

Ceri suddenly got to her feet, with some difficulty.

'Come with me!' she said. 'I'll introduce you to the rest of the backstage team. They'll find you something to do.'

I made to stand up, and stopped. Both of Ceri's legs were strapped up with black braces, from ankle to hips.

'What are those for?' I asked.

Ceri looked at me. 'Hmm? What?'

'Those things on your legs,' I said.

Ceri shrugged. 'Nothing. They help me walk.'

'Oh,' I said. 'Do you have to wear them all the time? They don't hurt or get in the way or anything?'

Ceri frowned. 'What, you mean like your stupid helmet?'

She pointed at it. I struggled to think of what to say.

'Er . . . I guess so,' I said.

Ceri smiled. 'No. They don't get in the way. Ever. Shall we?'

With that she turned around and marched off across the hall. I followed without protest. Ceri seemed pretty weird, but at least she was talking to me. And even better, she wasn't Callum.

'Hey, Orlaith – *Orlaith!*' she said, waving her arms frantically at a nearby table.

A girl behind it snapped round irritably. I recognised her – it was the one who had talked to me in class the day before. She had tied her hair up neatly on top of her head, or as neatly as she could manage. Even in the dark it looked pretty impossible to control. She still wasn't smiling.

'What,' she said irritably.

Ceri pointed at me. 'Orlaith, this is Owen. He's a

victim of Miss Pewlish's abusive performing arts regime. Mind if he sits with you?'

Orlaith sighed.

'*Fine*,' she said, though I sensed she didn't really mean it. 'So long as he keeps quiet. And doesn't touch the props.'

She nodded at the rows of complex contraptions covering every inch of the tabletop in front of her. Ceri immediately picked one up and turned it round in her hands, to Orlaith's obvious irritation.

'Orlaith made all these herself,' Ceri explained, holding out the prop. 'Aren't they amazing? She doesn't smile or make jokes or be friendly or anything, but she's probably a genius. She's even off to the Valley Academy next year!'

Orlaith glowered. 'Thanks.'

'You're welcome,' beamed Ceri.

'Hang on,' I said. 'Is that . . . a stormtrap?'

I pointed at the prop in Ceri's hand. It was a metal box with a red light on top – just like the one on top of the clock tower. It had obviously been built and painted by hand. Orlaith snatched it back.

'Of *course* it's a stormtrap,' she muttered. 'What else would it be?'

'It's amazing,' I said. 'Just like the real thing. What's it for?'

Orlaith pointed to the stage. A group of scientists were now standing in a line, each one holding one of Orlaith's handmade stormtraps. The boy playing the tornado swirled around them in a dramatic tinselly circles.

[NARRATOR steps forward.]

NARRATOR: Barrow quickly became famous as the safest village in the valleys! Soon it was even using high-tech science-y know-how to protect itself from dreaded tornado attacks.

[SCIENTISTS place the stormtraps on the ground and switch them on. The light bulbs on top flash and emit a high-pitched beeping sound. TORNADO suddenly stops dead in the middle of the stage.]

TORNADO: What? Nooooo! I'm being pushed away by these infernal machines!
SCIENTIST 1: The stormtraps are a success! Let's put one in every village!

[SCIENTISTS high-five each other. TORNADO sulks offstage.]

NARRATOR: And so Barrow gave the valleys its greatest invention: the stormtrap, capable of protecting villages from tornadoes. Most villages foolishly thought they'd be safe with just one! But not the people of Barrow.

[VILLAGERS *place the stormtraps in a great circle on stage.*]

NARRATOR: They surrounded their entire valley with a ring of stormtraps, protecting the village on every side. Now there was no way a tornado could *ever* harm them. [*Darkly*] Perhaps, if the other villages had protected their valleys properly, the terrible tragedy that was to come might never have happened . . .

I suddenly noticed that someone else was stood beside me in the dark. I turned to face him, and startled. It was the boy who had been waiting with Orlaith the day before. His enormous frame was now covered from head to toe in ragged brown fur, and a giant stuffed bear's head was placed over his own. He gazed down at me, his eyes blinking nervously between the bear's open jaws. Ceri leant forwards.

'Oh!' she said. 'I almost forgot to introduce you. Owen, this is Murderous Pe—'

Orlaith swung round on her chair, fixing Ceri with a warning glare. Ceri stumbled.

'Er . . . sorry, I mean *Big* Pete. He's Orlaith's Home-Time Partner.'

I held out my hand. 'Hello, Pete.'

Pete looked at me cautiously, and then extended a paw. He silently wrapped his entire enormous hand around mine.

'Hi,' he whispered.

Orlaith leant forwards between us, separating our hands jealously.

'Pete, that was your cue. Go get ready in the wings.'

Pete spun round obediently and scurried to the back of the stage. I watched him go, his enormous feet padding softly into the darkness of the hall.

'Wow!' I gulped. 'He's *huge*.'

Ceri nodded. 'Yep. Just *wait* till you see what he does in the play! It's incredible. But, er . . . make sure you don't get on his bad side.'

I looked at her blankly. 'What do you mean?'

Ceri stole a glance to see if Orlaith could hear her, and leant in to whisper.

'Pete's got a bit of a *violent reputation*,' she explained.

'That's why everyone calls him Murderous Pete. Last year he punched a kid so hard his brain came out of his ears. Oh, and once he made a boy in the year above eat his own arms.'

I gasped. 'You saw him do that?'

Ceri stared at me blankly. 'Er . . . well no, I didn't. But I do have some very good sources.'

'*Shhh!*' Orlaith hissed angrily. Onstage the play had reached its dramatic climax.

NARRATOR: . . . Until one terrible night, ten years ago, a tornado landed beside a careless village called High Folly . . .

[*TORNADO is swirling throughout the valleys, causing havoc. VILLAGERS OF HIGH FOLLY spill left, right and centre.*]

FOLLY VILLAGER 1: Oh no! Our village's single stormtrap isn't strong enough to protect us from the tornado!

FOLLY VILLAGER 2: If only we'd followed Barrow's shining example and installed several stormtraps instead of belittling their suggestions!

[*TORNADO smashes houses, statues, trees. A sign reading 'BEAR SANCTUARY' is lowered from the rafters.*]

FOLLY VILLAGER 1: Oh no! The tornado's heading straight for our poorly constructed Bear Sanctuary!

[*TORNADO smashes the sign, accompanied by another terrifying crash of cymbals.*]

FOLLY VILLAGER 1: Look! The bears are escaping!

[*From the darkness at the back of the stage, a single BEAR steps forwards into the light.*]
BEAR: Rooooooooooar.

[*BEAR suddenly grabs FOLLY VILLAGER 1 and lifts him straight off the ground, holding him above his head as if he was as light as a pillow. Everyone screams.*]

NARRATOR: What's he doing?!
FOLLY VILLAGER 1: Help! Miss Pewlish! Make him put me down, quick!

BEAR: [*fumbling*] S-sorry.

[BEAR drops FOLLY VILLAGER 1 and scurries offstage. FOLLY VILLAGERS follow him from a distance, pointing and whispering.]

NARRATOR: Since that terrible day ten years ago, the people of the valleys were struck with yet another threat – loose bears roaming the valleys at night, hunting disobedient and careless children still out on the streets. They are a constant reminder that we must always try to be safe and follow the Storm Laws – even when there are no tornadoes.

[THOMAS BARROW steps onstage.]

THOMAS BARROW: So remember, children – the Storm Laws are here to protect you! Always make sure you stay indoors during curfew!

[Lights suddenly dim.]

And if you don't want to follow the Storm Laws? Well – there's always plenty of room at the County Detention Centre.

[A child walks onstage, dressed as a MAN. The whole

room falls silent. The MAN wears a black suit, and has a shaved head, and wears black glasses that hide his eyes completely. He stands in the centre of the stage and does not move. The lights dim and dim, until all you can see is the MAN and nothing else, except the nametag that is clipped to his chest. It reads: THE WARDEN.]

THE WARDEN: And then you're mine.

The bell rang. Without another word everyone tore off their costumes and started racing out the doors. Ceri tapped me on the shoulder.

'Thanks for the interview, Owen,' she said, smiling broadly. 'See you tomorrow!'

She marched off across the hall. Orlaith glanced up from behind the table.

'Er . . . aren't you forgetting something, Ceri?'

Ceri turned round. 'Hmm? What?'

Orlaith sighed, and pointed to the corner. There, on a stool, sat a small girl eating a pencil case. She looked like a miniature version of Ceri, with white-blonde hair poking out beneath a woolly hat. Ceri rolled her eyes.

'*Flossie!*' said Ceri. 'There you are! Come on – it's home time.'

Ceri grabbed the little girl's hand and dragged her out

the exit. I turned round to say goodbye to Orlaith, but once again she had already disappeared. In her place stood Callum, glaring down at me. I startled helplessly.

'Ready?' he muttered gruffly.

I nodded, shivering the twitch out of my arms. Callum looked me up and down, and smirked.

'Better get you home quick,' he said. 'Don't want you to faint again, do we?'

He chuckled, and strode out the door. I watched him go, my blood boiling, but I swallowed my anger carefully. No matter what Callum said, I couldn't let anything go wrong on the walk home today. If he attacked me and I was late for curfew for the second day in a row, and my parents thought it was because I was trying to climb trees again . . . well, who *knows* how much trouble I'd be in then?

I scampered after him. Surely nothing bad would happen this time. Not two days in a row. Not if I didn't give him a reason. No one's that much of a bully – right?

5
Why I Broke the Storm Laws

Callum and I sat at the back of the classroom in silence. Every now and then one of the other children would turn around and look at me. They might have been looking at the mysterious shoebox I held in my lap, but judging by the look on their faces they were looking at the red stinging nettle welts that now covered me from head to toe.

'Can't believe you actually did a presentation,' Callum muttered.

I didn't reply. After yesterday's disastrous walk home, I had no desire to talk to Callum any more. I was going to ignore him, just like everyone else. We only had a few weeks left of being Home-Time Partners – I wasn't going to waste any of it trying to reason with him. You can't reason with a brick wall. Especially one that keeps pushing you into stinging nettles.

The bell rang. Miss Pewlish locked the door behind her and faced the class.

'Presentation Day!' she cried shrilly. 'Let's get started, shall we?' She riffled around on her desk. 'Let's see, who's first on the list – Brenner, Callum . . .'

'Haven't done it!' Callum chimed.

'. . . which brings us straight onto Dewbridge, Ceri,' said Miss Pewlish, barely missing a beat as she put a cross next to Callum's name. 'So Ceri, if you'd like to, er . . . take it away.'

Ceri slammed the PRESS hat onto her head and marched up to the front of the class with an enormous stack of paper. She dumped it on the floor and pointed at it dramatically.

'Read it and weep!' she cried. 'Another exclusive report by the *Dewbridge Gazette*! Revealing the appalling working conditions behind the scenes of Barrow Prep's so-called "celebration" of the life of Thomas Barrow, who I can now *sensationally reveal* . . .'

Miss Pewlish sighed.

'Of course,' she said. 'A damning exposé. Just like last week. And the week before.' She rubbed her temples.

'Tell you what, Ceri – how about I give you a "B+", and you can just sit back down?'

Ceri thought about it. 'Er . . . alright.'

We applauded politely as Ceri sat back down. Miss Pewlish wiped her brow with relief.

One by one, each child went up to the front. Everyone had something to present on, whether it be a favourite book or a piece of artwork they had done. Orlaith did hers on a burglar alarm system she had built herself, which sprayed intruders with month-old mayonnaise from head to toe when they stepped on a specially rigged doormat. Even Murderous Pete got up and did a presentation on a teapot he had brought from home, although he didn't say much except that it was a teapot and then stood there in silence for the remaining two minutes. He still got a round of applause, although I suspected this was because everyone was frightened of what he'd do to them if they didn't clap.

Finally, there was only one presentation left to go.

'Underwood,' said Miss Pewlish. 'Underwood, Owen.'

I carried my shoebox to the front, stomach churning, and faced the class. They all sat, sparkly eyed, waiting for me to startle and smash a priceless antique vase or something. I steeled myself. I was sick of being a joke. I wasn't going to give them the satisfaction.

'My presentation is on my grandparents,' I said.

There was an audible groan from the back of the classroom that everyone ignored.

'I never met them,' I said. 'They died before I was born. Back when they were alive, though, everyone in the valleys knew who they were. They were famous.'

I put the box on the floor, and opened the lid.

'My grandparents were called "The Tornado Chasers",' I said.

I pulled out a brown leather helmet from inside the box, and held it up. The whole class murmured with interest. The helmet had ear flaps, and a fur trim, and pilot goggles attached to the front that had been smashed many years ago. Across the side, still visible despite its age, was a picture of a spiralling tornado, the shadow of a bi-plane emblazoned across it. Underneath, stitched in rolling script, read the initials: 'T.C.'

'They were pilots,' I explained. '*Daredevil* pilots. They used to fly stunts for shows, doing loop-the-loops and flying right over the audiences' heads and stuff.'

Everyone cooed. Miss Pewlish shuffled nervously in her chair.

'Well, that certainly sounds very *dangerous*, Owen . . .'

'Oh, it was,' I said, nodding. 'Incredibly dangerous. There weren't many people around back then who did what they did, and they were the best in the business. My grandmother even did a thing called "wing walking", where she'd walk across the wings of the plane while it was in the air.'

I pulled out a pile of black-and-white photos from the box, and started handing them round. The class gasped in amazement. The photos showed a plane in mid-flight, taken from the ground, my grandmother's shadow on the wings cast against the sun.

'Pretty exciting stuff,' I said. 'But that wasn't the reason they were famous. That was because of something else they did. Something *much* more dangerous.'

I paused, and looked up. The entire class was staring back at me in anticipation.

'You see,' I said, 'they were always trying to be even more daring, to really push themselves. So they started a club called "The Tornado Chasers", with some other daredevil pilots. It was a secret club. You couldn't tell anyone that you were a member. Because actually, what they were doing was *life-threatening*.'

Miss Pewlish shifted uncomfortably on her chair. 'Er . . .'

'Whenever a tornado landed in the valley,' I said, meeting the eyes of my classmates, 'and everyone else had shut themselves up safely at home – the Tornado Chasers would leap in their planes, and fly straight towards it!'

The whole class gasped in shock, including Miss Pewlish.

53

'They knew it was dangerous,' I said. 'But that was kind of the whole point – to do something that no one else would ever *dream* of doing. There used to be lots of tornadoes back then. There weren't even any stormtraps to protect the villages – they hadn't been invented yet. People were really frightened. But not my grandparents. They even had a motto: "We are the Tornado Chasers, and we are not afraid" . . .'

'Lovely, Owen,' said Miss Pewlish, getting out of her seat. 'Well, I think that's quite enough for today . . .'

'Until one day,' I continued, pulling out a newspaper from the box, 'it all ended in tragedy.'

I held up the newspaper, and the whole class gasped again. The cover was taken up by a giant photo of a shattered plane, hung upside down in a tree. It was surrounded by a circle of solemn policemen, their heads bowed. A helmet hung down from the cockpit by a torn strap.

'One day a tornado touched down,' I said, 'and they flew out to meet it as usual. All five – my grandfather, my grandmother, and the three other Tornado Chasers – disappeared. No one knows what happened to them. Their bodies were never found. They figured the tornado just changed direction unexpectedly, and they couldn't get away in time.'

Miss Pewlish sighed with relief, and sat back down.

'Of course,' she said. 'A fitting end to such reckless and unsafe activity! It should be a lesson to all of you. Thank you, Owen, that was a very . . .'

'But before I finish,' I said quickly, 'I'd like to show you all this.'

I reached right down to the bottom of the box, and fished out a framed picture. I turned it round to the class.

'It's a photo of the tornado,' I said. 'Taken from the plane as they were flying beside it. That's how close they used to get.'

The class looked in awe at the photo in my hands. The background was a blur, a hundred mile-an-hour vortex of rocks, trees, whole houses, everything the tornado could tear up from the ground, a solid wall of wind that filled the frame from edge to edge. But right in the centre of the photo, strapped onto the wing of the plane, was a woman. Her mouth was open. Her hair whipped around her face, and she held up her arms to the sky. I tapped my finger on the glass.

'*That's* my grandmother,' I said. 'Wing walking beside the tornado. My grandfather took it himself from the cockpit.' I smiled. 'It's my favourite photo.'

I held it for a moment, and looked up. The whole class was whispering excitedly and nudging each other. To my surprise, Callum was staring at the photo, too. His mouth was hanging open, and his eyes were glimmering. It was almost uncomfortable to look at.

'Er . . . thanks,' I said.

The whole class burst into applause. Miss Pewlish glanced at them nervously.

'Quieten down, everyone,' she muttered. 'Quieten down please.'

I smiled. It was a good feeling.

■ ■ ■

'Hey, Owen! *Owen!*'

Ceri caught me as I was halfway out the door. I startled, and it immediately slammed back into my face.

'*Amazing* presentation this morning!' said Ceri, appearing not to notice.

'Thanks,' I said, rubbing my nose. The presentation had certainly been a success. Miss Pewlish had given me one of the highest marks in the class, largely to stop the class from cheering when I had finished.

'Your grandmother was an absolute legend,' said Ceri. 'Standing on the wing of a plane! Unbelievable! And your granddad was pretty nifty with a camera too, if I say so myself. Any idea what type of camera or lenses he was using? I do a bit of photography too, you know.'

'Er . . . no, sorry,' I said. 'I guess I could find out, though. My parents still have all their old equipment at home.'

Ceri's face lit up. 'That'd be great! How about you bring it all round to mine after school tomorrow? I'd love to interview you about your grandparents for the next *Dewbridge Gazette*. You'd have to stay the night for curfew, but I'm sure my parents would be fine with it. They're pretty relaxed. They're letting me make salad tomorrow.'

I beamed. 'Sure! Let's—'

I stopped, and my face fell.

'Actually, I can't,' I said despondently. 'My parents have grounded me for a week because they think I can't stop climbing trees.'

'Oh,' said Ceri.

She paused.

'*Are* you climbing trees?'

'No,' I said miserably.

She thought about it for a moment, and then shrugged.

'OK,' she said. 'Well, let me know if they change their minds. See you tomorrow!'

She made her way across the playground, walking straight past the little girl who stood waiting for her at the bottom of the steps.

'Er . . . Ceri?' I called after her. 'Isn't that your sister?'

I pointed to the girl, who was eating yoghurt out of a pot by mashing it against her face with her mouth open. Ceri rolled her eyes.

'*Flossie!*' She sighed. 'Not again! Honestly, she gets lost like, every single day.'

She grabbed Flossie's hand and dragged her across the green, gurgling. I turned to walk after her, and stopped. Callum was staring up at me from the bottom of the steps. He shook his head.

'You,' he said, 'were going to go round a girl's house.' He paused. 'For *salad*.'

I walked straight past him. I wasn't going to get tricked into talking to him again – not today. He quickly caught up with me, waiting for a reaction. I gave him nothing.

'So,' he said, after a moment of silence. 'That thing about your grandparents was sort of OK. It wasn't as bad as the other presentations, I mean.'

I didn't reply.

'Er . . .' said Callum. 'What were they called again?'

'The Tornado Chasers,' I said curtly.

Callum nodded. 'Yeah. "Tornado Chasers". That's, yeah . . . really, really cool.'

We crossed the bridge and walked beside the stream in silence. I picked up the pace. I wasn't going to let him make me late again.

'That's the sort of thing I'd do, you know,' said Callum, apparently under the impression we were having a conversation. 'If I could be bothered. Run out of the village and chase a storm, take some pictures of it. Like it's no big deal.'

'Really,' I said.

'Yeah.' Callum grinned. 'That'd show all the idiots around here.' His face darkened. 'I'll tell you what, they wouldn't think I was such a big joke any more . . . Going on about me like I'm a *baby*, just because I got kept back a year!' He growled. 'I'd like to see the looks on their faces when they saw a photo of me, standing right next to a . . .'

He stopped mid-sentence, and fell silent. I turned round. He was fixed to the spot, staring into the middle distance. The corners of his mouth slowly flickered up into a smile.

'That's it,' he muttered. 'That's how I'll show them! I'll be a . . . what were they called again?'

'Tornado Chaser,' I said dryly.

'Yeah!' he said. 'A Tornado Chaser! I'll sneak out the village and run after a tornado! I'll be famous! The hardest boy in Barrow – in all the valleys, even!'

A ray of sunlight cut through the trees and lit up his face. He was beaming.

'Great,' I said, turning away from him. 'Well, good luck with that.'

59

Callum glared at me. 'I mean it! I'll really do it! And I'll take pictures to prove it, too.'

'I'm sure you will,' I said politely over my shoulder.

Callum glowered.

'Well, who cares what you think?' he said, running to catch up with me. 'It's because of having a dweebus like *you* as my Home-Time Partner that I have to do it in the first place!'

I blinked defensively. 'Well, I'm *not* a dweebus actually, so . . .'

Callum snorted. 'Oh, of course not! You're a regular tough guy, aren't you? That's why you can't go to Ceri's tomorrow night – because of all that "tree-climbing" you've been doing after school?'

I flashed crimson.

'Er . . . well,' I mumbled hopelessly. 'I mean, my parents are quite strict about that sort of thing, and . . .'

'Well, they don't need to be!' said Callum. 'You? Climb trees? *As if!*'

I shot him a furious glance.

'For your information,' I muttered, 'I am *extremely* good at climbing trees. I used to do it all the time. I was the best in Skirting. Then one day . . . well, my parents caught me doing it, and I startled. So I fell and hit my head. It's why I have to wear the helmet. It's not because I'm a . . . a *dweebus*.'

'Alright then,' said Callum, taking a step forwards. 'Seeing as you're such an expert tree-climber, we'll have a test.'

'Fine!' I said.

'It'll decide, once and for all, whether or not you're a big fat liar. And the biggest wuss in the world.'

'Fine!' I said. 'Name the time and I'll be there!'

'Tomorrow after school,' said Callum. 'After curfew's started.'

My eyelids barely flickered.

'A-after curfew?' I squeaked.

'Yep,' said Callum. He glanced at me casually. 'That's not a problem, is it?'

I broke out into a cold sweat.

'No,' I said, shaking my head, 'of course it isn't.'

Callum looked me up and down, and grinned. 'You mean it? You'll break curfew and everything? You're *really* going to do it?'

I looked at him. Was I really going to do it? Was I really prepared to lie to my parents, break the Storm Laws, risk being sent to the County Detention Centre, and possibly even get eaten alive by bears – *just* to climb a tree and prove Callum wrong?

6

How I Became a Tornado Chaser

Callum patted the tree beside him.

'*This*,' he said, 'is the tallest tree in Barrow.'

I gazed up the tree. Then I wished I hadn't. It was twice as tall as the one I fell out of in Skirting. The trunk was thin and wobbly, the topmost branches swaying perilously in the wind that blew down the valley. It was getting stronger and stronger every day now. I was quickly regretting yesterday's snap decision. Callum strolled towards me.

'Seeing as you're so *extremely* good at tree-climbing,' said Callum, a grin spreading across his face, '*you* are going to climb it. Right now. The whole thing. Every – last – branch.'

I looked up at the tree again. I'd never tried to climb

one like this before. The branches didn't even look strong enough to hold my weight.

'Are you . . . are you sure we have time?' I said nervously.

Callum nodded. 'Of course! Curfew doesn't start for another five minutes! Besides, you organised your cover story – right?'

I had. I'd told my parents that my presentation had got the highest mark in class, before asking if I could stay the next night at Ceri's as a reward. It was a risky strategy, but it had worked. After promising them that I would wear my knee-pads and sterilise the salad before I ate it, they had relented. After the test was over, I'd stay the night at Callum's. It was foolproof. Which meant that there was no way I could get out of it now. I could have kicked myself.

'Off you go then, Fearless Owen,' said Callum, strolling back to the tree and leaning against it casually. 'Let's see how brave you *really* are!'

I gulped, and made my way to the base of the tree. The remains of a sawn-off stump lay just above my head. I gripped it in one hand, and slowly pulled myself up onto the first branch. I got to my feet, and tried to balanced myself. My legs suddenly wobbled, and I had to grip onto the trunk of the tree.

'What a great start!' said Callum, applauding loudly. 'I certainly hope nothing goes wrong!'

I grit my teeth. I wasn't going to let myself be humiliated again – not by him. I looked ahead. There was another branch just ahead of me, slightly higher up. In a snap I vaulted over to it, grabbing the trunk again for support as I landed.

'Hey,' I heard Callum say from below. 'Not bad.'

Without a pause I grabbed the next branch above and swung myself onto it, before using the trunk to shimmy up another few feet and elegantly leap onto the branch above that. I glanced down. Callum was staring up, open-mouthed.

'Whoa,' he said quietly.

I grinned. 'I *told* you I was good.'

I looked around. I could do this. Halfway up to the next branch was a knothole, big enough for my foot. I wrapped my arms around the trunk and wedged my foot inside it. Now, all I had to do was push myself up and reach out to . . .

'STOP THAT AT ONCE!' cried an angry voice from the ground below.

I startled. My legs sprang out like pistons and catapulted me away from the tree like a squirrel, and sent me plummeting to the ground. Fortunately my fall was broken by the patch of stinging nettles at the bottom.

I leapt up, skin on fire. A yellow car was parked in the

clearing behind us, the words BARROW TRUANCY OFFICER marked out in big black letters on the side. In front of it stood a man in a bright yellow uniform. He had dark wiry hair, hard eyes, and a mean face. He was staring at me furiously.

'*Well?*' he barked. 'What the hell do you two think you're doing out here?'

I mouthed hopelessly. Answers, explanations, excuses, all evaporated to dust in my mouth. I had no idea what I could possibly say. Callum suddenly leapt forward.

'Why, Officer Reade!' he cried. 'What a surprise! I was just on my way home, actually, and er . . . got a bit lost . . .'

'You live on Magnolia Crescent, Brenner,' the man growled, swinging round to face him. 'The other side of the village. Care to explain what you're doing here *two minutes* before curfew is due to start?'

Callum slapped his face with shock.

'Two minutes!' he gasped. 'Well, I'd better get going right away, then! Thanks for your help, Officer Reade . . .'

He made to walk away, but the man threw him a furious glare and Callum stopped in his tracks. The man looked him over as one would a dead rat in a trap, before turning back to me. I squirmed hopelessly in the light of his mean eyes. I couldn't shake the feeling that he seemed somehow . . . familiar.

'Do you know who I am?' said the man.

I shook my head. The man stepped forwards.

'I'm Officer Reade,' he said. 'The Barrow Truancy Officer. That means that I'm the one who makes sure children in Barrow are either in school or at home.'

I tried to ignore how much my legs were shaking, and the sickening hot-cold floods that were swelling up inside me.

'And *yet*,' he said, throwing a glance at Callum, 'while I'm patrolling the village on my afternoon rounds, I find two children – two of my own daughter's classmates! – walking around outside and climbing trees.' He paused dramatically. '*Trees! Outside!* During an *SW5*!'

Callum and I squirmed.

'Do you have any idea how dangerous it is out here?' Officer Reade cried, the pitch of his voice getting higher and higher. 'The tornado could land any time! Bears are going to start roaming the valleys soon! Do you want to end up dead? Or in hospital? Or in the *County Detention Centre*?' He darted his eyes between us. 'Well, *do you*? Because that's where you two are headed, as far as I'm concerned. Let's see if you can explain to the Warden himself what you've been up to. Ha! I'm sure he'll be *very* interested!'

At the mere mention of the name, Callum let out a little squeak. His face had turned pale.

The clock tower in the distance suddenly chimed –
once, twice, three, four times.

'Curfew's started,' snapped Officer Reade. He folded
his arms. 'So unless you have a *very* good reason to
be here, then I'm taking the two of you home and
explaining to your parents what happened.'

I floundered, my mouth gaping and shutting like a
fish on the floor of a boat. That was it. I was done for.
My parents were going to kill me.

'I . . .'

'*The Dewbridges*'!' Callum suddenly cried, leaping
forwards.

Officer Reade looked at him in surprise. I stared at
Callum as he flailed his arms wildly.

'He's supposed to be staying the night at Ceri
Dewbridge's!' he said. 'That's why we came this way!
Owen forgot he was supposed to go to hers tonight, and
he didn't know how to get there, so I said I'd show him
myself because he's new, and we cut through the woods
so I could get back in time, but we got lost, and so Owen
said he'd climb a tree and find the quickest way out the
forest, and . . .'

'That true?' said Officer Reade, turning to me.

I nodded violently. Officer Reade kept his gaze fixed
on me for a moment, before turning to Callum.

'And you?' he said. 'Where are your parents?'

Callum paused, and scuffed the ground with his foot. 'They're . . . they're out of town for the week.'

Officer Reade nodded. 'Your babysitter at home?'

Callum glowered at him. 'She's not my babysi—'

Officer Reade made a growling noise in his throat, and Callum stopped. He looked at the two of us for a while longer, his brain ticking slowly over, his mean eyes flitting between us.

'That was a *very* unsafe idea,' he said eventually. 'So consider this a warning. Take him to Ceri's, and then go straight back to yours. Understand?'

Callum nodded quickly. Officer Reade turned back to his car. Then he stopped, and glanced over his shoulder at me.

'You should probably get out of those nettles,' he said. I looked down. Maybe it was the fear, or the adrenaline of plummeting twenty feet to the ground, but I had somehow forgotten that I was standing chest-deep in stinging nettles. I clambered out. Officer Reade stepped back into his car, and quickly sped off through the trees. Callum and I stood in the billowing dust left by the wheels, watching him disappear.

Callum waited until all was silent. Then he picked up a dead branch from the ground and threw it in the general direction of where Officer Reade's car had headed. It landed with a thump five feet away. Callum turned round in triumph.

'Ha!' he bellowed. 'That showed him!'

I pulled a strand of stinging nettles from out of my helmet with red raw fingers. I couldn't get Officer Reade's face out of my head.

'That man,' I said. 'He looked . . . he looked just like . . .'

Callum nodded. 'Yep! He's *Orlaith's dad*. Can you believe it? No wonder she's such a dork! He's the one who makes sure nobody leaves their house once curfew starts. He even drives around the village every single night, making sure no one's on the streets. Honestly, he thinks he's so hard. Everyone around here's frightened of him.'

'But not you,' I said.

'Yeah, not me,' said Callum. 'Obviously.' He paused. 'So, er . . . yeah. You're in, I guess.'

I looked back at him. 'Pardon?'

Callum scratched the back of his head. 'My gang. The Tornado Chasers. You passed the test. I suppose you're in now.'

I looked confused. 'But I wasn't trying to be in your . . .'

'Yeah, well,' said Callum. 'You seem to be able to take

a lot of injuries without dying, and that could be pretty useful if I ever need a human shield. Might as well let you in, seeing as you're so desperate for it. It'll shut you up about it at least.'

'Er . . . thanks,' I said.

Callum held out a hand.

'Welcome to the gang,' he said.

I gazed at Callum. For all his faults – and there were lots of them – I had to admit that I'd never met anyone quite like him before. He was big and mean and full of rubbish, but then so are garbage trucks – and they're pretty hard to ignore when they're charging full speed ahead. And he had something I couldn't put my finger on. I'd have *never* thought up starting up the Tornado Chasers again. It was all Callum's idea, from the very beginning. Maybe he really was brave. Then again, maybe he was just stupid.

Either way, only an *idiot* would have agreed to join a plan that was so clearly ridiculous. And unrealistic. And dangerous.

And exciting.

I took his hand.

'The Tornado Chasers,' I said.

7

How Two Became Five

'Everyone off the bus!' cried Miss Pewlish. 'Stick with your partners!'

Callum and I clambered outside and stood in front of the zoo gates. It was pretty hard for us not to stick with each other, seeing as we were tied together with bits of rope.

'Stupid Storm Laws,' Callum grumbled, picking at our bound wrists. 'Can't believe we have to go on this stupid surprise trip.'

I shrugged. 'Well, it's nice to be out at least. I never would have thought they'd let us leave the classroom during an *SW5*.'

Callum nodded. 'Yeah . . . Weird.'

I gave him a glance. 'Plus, it means we don't have to watch that stupid play again.'

Callum laughed. 'Ha! Yeah, exactly!'

He suddenly stopped, and we glanced at each other. It was the first time I'd heard Callum laugh when he wasn't laughing *at* me. There was an awkward silence as the rest of the children filed out the bus behind us.

'So – everything go OK at Ceri's yesterday?' he muttered. 'Her parents didn't rat on you, did they?'

I shook my head. Thankfully Ceri's parents had believed my terrible excuses for turning up at their house without warning. After they had supervised Ceri making the salad and made us both wash our hands several times, they had left us well alone so Ceri could interview me about my grandparents. It was – well, it was fun.

A loud whistle suddenly silenced the crowd, and we swung round. Miss Pewlish was stood beside a stone wall up ahead. The wall dropped down into a deep pit. It was just big enough for a child to look over, and was lined on every side with enormous red warning signs. Miss Pewlish fixed us with a beady eye.

'We have been invited here today,' she said, 'for a *very important purpose*. It's not often the Warden allows groups outside during an SW5! It is so that you children can understand the very real, and the very *frightening* threat of bear attacks once the tornado has landed.'

Miss Pewlish took a moment to clear her throat.

'During a storm,' she said, 'when whole houses are ripped from the ground and villages destroyed, you'd think that bears would want to hide in their caves for safety . . . but you'd be wrong. You see, the tornadoes scatter all their other sources of food. The starving bears are forced to roam the valleys even more than usual. And when this happens, their primary source of food is reckless young children, wandering the streets at night on their own.'

Callum shuffled his feet nervously beside me.

'That is why,' Miss Pewlish declared, 'while the valleys are under SW5, it is *even more* important that you stick to the rules of the curfew. Barrow might be the safest village in the valleys, but the stormtraps won't stop a hungry bear from waiting outside your bedroom window! Would *you* like to turn a corner and find this waiting for you?'

Miss Pewlish stepped aside, and a gasp escaped the crowd. In the centre of the enclosure, in amongst the tufts of grass and stagnant blocks of still water, a single bear lay slumped asleep. It was very old. Its brown fur was shedding and patched with grey, and its huge chest billowed weakly with grunting breaths you could only just hear over the terrified whispers around us. It didn't matter that the bear was old, or asleep. It didn't even matter that there was a wall between us. It was a bear, the greatest threat in the valleys. No one felt safe.

'Everyone line up!' Miss Pewlish barked. 'Each child will take turns looking at the bear! By order of the Warden!'

I felt a sudden tug on my wrist. Callum was heaving at the rope linking us, his face turned away from me.

'Let's go,' he said. 'This is boring.'

'We can't leave,' I said. 'Don't you remember what Miss Pewlish said on the bus? We can't leave the crowd or . . .'

'She's an idiot,' said Callum, his voice suddenly striking a higher pitch than normal. 'Come on, I need to talk to you. It's important.'

I frowned. 'About what?'

Callum groaned. 'What do you think? *The gang*, stupid.'

I beamed. *The gang*. I was actually in a gang, for the first time in my life. I wasn't exactly thrilled that it was with Callum, but that didn't really matter. I was finally going to be a daredevil – just like my grandparents. And climbing trees was *nothing* compared to what we had planned.

Callum dragged me to a secluded spot at the back of the crowd, and leant in to whisper.

'So, here's what I was thinking,' he said. 'We're going to need a hideout. A top-secret one. My mum and dad are away almost all the time so the house is pretty empty, but then my babysit . . . er, I mean, my *cleaner*'s always there looking after me. And we can't go to yours because your parents are clearly mental.'

I blinked. 'They are?'

'But get this,' said Callum excitedly. 'I've got a storm shelter in my back garden! A proper one, made of metal – it's underground and everything. It'd be perfect – no one would ever think to look down there! Not even Officer Reade. And let's face it Owen, that's the *last* thing we want. That's why we can't tell anyone about our plans, obviously.'

My stomach dropped.

'We . . . we can't?' I muttered.

'Course not!' said Callum. 'We don't want any losers or wimps wanting to get involved, do we? This gang's for the bravest. The strongest. The hardest.'

'Of . . . of course,' I squeaked. 'But say, one of us accidentally mentioned it to someone else, say last night for example, and then . . .'

'And on that subject,' said Callum, cutting me off. 'There's one person I think we *should* invite.' He quickly checked no one was listening, and leant in even closer. '. . . *Murderous Pete*.'

I almost leapt back in surprise.

'*Murderous Pete?*' I said. 'Isn't he supposed to be a psychopath?'

Callum shrugged. 'Well, yeah. But a psychopath in our gang could be pretty useful. You know, in case we have to fight off any bears while we're out chasing the tornado. I'm the leader, after all. I can't afford to get my hands dirty.' He tugged at my wrist. 'Come on, let's enrol him now!'

He dragged me into the crowd before I could protest any further. Finding Pete was easy – he towered over the crowd like a brick wall. Orlaith stood at his side, tied to his wrist. Callum jabbed her shoulder and she spun round. Her face immediately took on the look of someone opening the fridge to find nothing but a pint of old milk and a raw fish.

'What,' she muttered.

'We need to talk to Murderous Pete,' said Callum.

Orlaith fumed. 'His name is *not* . . .'

'Blah blah blah, whatever,' Callum snapped. 'Come on, we've got business with him and it doesn't concern you! Go invent a machine that shuts you up for ten minutes. Something everyone can enjoy.'

Orlaith considered saying something, then just turned her back to us, shaking her head and muttering.

Callum turned round to Murderous Pete, who gazed back down at him blankly. I wondered if he was going to rip Callum's head off and start playing basketball with it. Callum's eyes suddenly flooded with panic. He pushed me forwards.

'Go on, Owen,' he squeaked. 'Tell nice Mr Pete about the plan.'

I looked up at Pete. It was like looking up the tree the day before, except this one could stamp your head into butter.

'Er . . . Hi Pete,' I said. 'Well, we're over here because Callum and I were thinking about starting up a gang. Remember the Tornado Chasers? The ones from my presentation the other day?'

Pete stared at me. His brow unfurrowed, ever so slightly.

'You mean . . . like in those planes you said about?' he said. His gentle voice always surprised me.

I smiled with relief. '*Yes!* That's it! Well done, Pete!'

I stepped forwards.

'We'd like you to join us. We're going to have meetings in Callum's storm shelter, and when the storm lands we're going to break out of the village and chase after it. We're going to be daredevils. Real-life daredevils, Pete!'

It felt exciting just to say it. Even my heart was beating

faster. All my life I'd wanted to be like my grandparents – to laugh in the face of danger, to live without fear. And now here I was, planning to break the Storm Laws, and dodge bears, and chase a tornado, and . . .

'That's a terrible idea.'

Our heads shot round. Orlaith was shaking her head beside us, deeply unimpressed.

'Oi!' said Callum. 'Why are you listening? This is none of your business!'

'How are you going to do it?' asked Orlaith.

Callum stumbled. 'Er . . . what?'

'*How* are you going to chase a tornado?' said Orlaith. 'You don't have planes.'

Callum was scuppered. 'Er . . .'

We looked at each other. We hadn't really thought about that bit yet. Callum's eyes suddenly lit up.

'We'll run!' he said triumphantly.

Orlaith nodded. 'Oh, *right*! You'll run after it. Well, *that's* a load off my mind. For a moment I thought you two didn't have a clue what you were doing.'

Callum eyed her suspiciously. 'That had better not be sarcasm.'

Orlaith sighed, and turned to Pete.

'Pete,' she said. 'I'm not going to let you be led along by these two morons.' She held up the rope that connected their wrists. 'If Pete's in, I'm in too.'

Callum took a step towards her. 'Oh, are you now? Says *who*?'

'Says my dad,' said Orlaith, stepping forwards to meet him. '*That's* who. As long as he's patrolling the streets, you can forget ever getting out of Barrow.' She cleared her throat. 'Unless, of course, you have someone in your gang who knows his routes round the village each night. Who knows how to get past him. Me.'

I glanced at Callum.

'She . . . she's got a pretty good point, Callum,' I said. 'You saw what her dad's like.'

Callum's eyes widened. He looked hopelessly from Orlaith to me, and then back again. His eyes struggled to process whatever was going on in his head. Finally he threw up his hands with frustration.

'Fine!' he cried. 'Whatever! She can be in this stupid gang if she has to be, I don't even care about it! God!'

Orlaith beamed. 'Glad to hear it. What shall we say: first meeting tomorrow afternoon? We might as well use your storm shelter, Callum. So long as your babysitter doesn't notice us.'

Callum trembled with frustration, and smacked me on the helmet.

'Nice one, idiot!' he hissed. ' "Oh, let's go invite Pete"

. . . great idea that turned out to be! Any more of your *loser* friends you want to tell about our top-secret gang while you're at it?'

'Oh, what,' said a voice behind us, 'you mean the Tornado Chasers?'

I froze. Callum froze.

We turned round. Behind us stood Ceri, calmly changing a lens on her camera. Flossie stood linked to her wrist, weighed down with several bags of camera equipment.

'W . . . what did you say?' Callum managed to choke out.

Ceri looked up. 'Your gang. The Tornado Chasers. The one Owen told me about in our interview last night.'

I had already started trying to scramble away, but Callum wrenched me back. He was making short spluttering noises, like the type an engine makes before it explodes and kills everybody.

'He . . . told you . . . about it?' he croaked.

Ceri snorted. 'Well, of course he did! He invited me to join the gang.' She frowned. 'Wait – that's the right word, isn't it? "Gang"? I think that's right . . .'

The ground swallowed me up. Or rather, I wish it had. At least then Callum wouldn't have been able to start using me as a human maraca.

'I'm sorry!' I cried as he shook me. 'I didn't realise we

weren't supposed to tell people!'

Ceri leant in between us, completely unaware that anything was the matter.

'Great!' she said. 'So, when's our first meeting? How about in Callum's storm shelter? You know, when his babysitter's not looking.'

Without warning Callum spun round and lunged hard, shoving her backwards. Ceri stumbled, her leg braces scraping on the dusty cobbles. She glanced up angrily.

'Hey!' she said.

'There *is* no first meeting!' said Callum. 'Not for you!'

A gust of wind suddenly picked up across the zoo, blowing hard against us. Ceri stepped forwards.

'*Why not?*' she demanded.

I glanced around nervously. Miss Pewlish was nowhere to be seen.

'Because,' Callum shouted, 'it's for the bravest, and the strongest! It's for people who aren't frightened of anything! And look at you . . . for God's sake, you can't even *walk* properly!'

It silenced us. No one knew what to say. Ceri stared at Callum, shifting the weight on her legs.

'I'm ten times stronger and braver than you, Callum,' she muttered.

Callum let out a bitter laugh. 'Oh you are, are you?

Go on then, prove it!'

He turned around and jabbed a finger into the bear enclosure.

'Climb inside that pen then, seeing as you're so *brave*,' he said. 'Go on! Let's all see you do it!'

Callum turned to us with a triumphant grin. We stared at him in silence. He placed his hands on his hips, reminding us exactly who was in charge. Then he spun back round to Ceri.

'And if you mention this in your *stupid* paper . . .'

He trailed off. Ceri had disappeared. In her place stood Flossie, sucking on a short length of rope that dangled from her wrist. It had been cut.

'Huh?' said Callum.

'CERI DEWBRIDGE!'

We all spun round. Miss Pewlish was sprinting towards us, holding a fresh cappuccino.

'GET OUT OF THERE!'

We looked at each other in confusion. Then we turned, and slowly looked over the wall of the enclosure. Our stomachs dropped.

Ceri was climbing on top of the sleeping bear.

'GET OFF THAT THING AT ONCE!' Miss Pewlish screamed. *'YOU HEAR ME? AT ONCE!'*

Ceri ignored her, and kept climbing. The bear wriggled

weakly beneath her, grumbling lazily before falling back asleep. Handful by handful Ceri heaved herself across its back and onto its shoulders. In one quick movement she slung her leg braces over the blades of its back, and sat upright to face the crowd.

There was not a single sound to be heard in the zoo now. The entire school stood packed around the wall of the bear enclosure, watching in disbelief at what was unfolding before them. A brace of wind blew down from the valleys and carried across the silent crowd. Ceri sat carefully balanced on the bear's shoulders, facing the sea of stunned faces. She took a moment to take it all in, her chest heaving. For a moment, even she looked surprised that she had done it.

And then she threw back her head, and punched the air with both hands.

'I,' she cried, *'am a Tornado Chaser!'*

She paused, letting the sound of her voice carry over the crowd and echo off the enclosure walls. Then, she very slowly turned to face Callum, her eyes triumphant. She pointed straight at him.

'And I am not *afraid!'*

8

How to Get Out of Serious Trouble

Miss Pewlish crossed her hands over the desk.

'So,' she said. 'One of you might as well tell me how it happened.'

We sat before her in grim silence. We had only just arrived back from the zoo. Orlaith and Pete were still tied at the wrist. Ceri was smeared grey with dust and moulting bear fur. Callum and I guiltily twiddled our thumbs. No one spoke.

'Anyone?' said Miss Pewlish.

We looked at each other in despair. In the chaos that had followed the bear incident, not one of us had thought to organise a cover story. There was no way we'd be able to make up an explanation now, without the risk of one of us slipping up and giving away the truth about the Tornado Chasers. And if anyone found out about that . . . well, we really were done for.

Miss Pewlish sighed, and shook her head.

'Never,' she said, her voice taut with anger, 'in all my years as School Safety Officer, have I *ever* come across such reckless or dangerous behaviour. On a school trip. *During an SW5!*' She slammed her hands on the tabletop, making us jump. 'You do realise that a tornado could have landed today, don't you?'

We cringed.

'You leave me no choice,' she muttered. 'With the power invested in me as School Safety Officer, I'm suspending all five of you – for the rest of the year. Your parents will be informed immediately.'

My stomach heaved.

'N-no,' I managed to croak. 'Not my parents!'

Miss Pewlish nodded sadly. 'Yes, Owen. And what's more, this incident will be recorded on all of your permanent files.'

Orlaith suddenly leapt from her seat.

'You . . . you can't,' she cried, her face desperate. 'I'm supposed to be going to the Valley Academy next year! They'll never take me with a suspension on my record!'

Miss Pewlish smiled coldly. 'I'm afraid that's not my

problem, Miss Reade. As School Safety Officer, I have a duty to uphold the Storm Laws which all five of you violated today.'

Ceri suddenly looked up, her eyes glimmering.

'We did?' she said. 'Which ones?'

Miss Pewlish's lip thinned. She heaved a giant book from under the desk and slammed it open on the table, jabbing a finger onto the page.

'*Inciting public disorder*,' she read. '*Endangering personal safety. Improper use of bears* . . . I could go on. And in an SW5 all Storm Laws – no matter how small – *must* be upheld.'

Ceri looked delighted. 'Really? *All* of them?'

Miss Pewlish glared at her stonily. 'Yes, Ceri! *All* of them!'

'Including Storm Law IX.ii?' said Ceri. 'The one that says a teacher on an outdoors field trip should be with her class at all times, and not buying a cappuccino from the zoo cafe?'

Miss Pewlish's face fell. 'I . . . I beg your pardon?'

Ceri stood up and leant over the desk, pointing at the book in front of her.

'It's just there, Miss Pewlish. Storm Law IX.ii: *Elected adults must take full responsibility for the children placed in their care at all times*. That elected adult would be . . .

you, in this case. Which means that sneaking off to grab a frothy coffee when on a school trip violates a Storm Law, too.'

Miss Pewlish fumbled.

'That's . . . beside the point,' she muttered. 'Several children saw the five of you arguing before convincing Ceri to climb inside that enclosure. And unless one of you has a *very* good explanation for that . . .'

'*Abandonment!*' I suddenly cried, leaping to my feet.

Everyone turned to look at me. I cleared my throat. I had to admit that I didn't really know what I was doing.

'I . . . I saw what happened to Ceri beside the bear enclosure,' I said. 'When you left, Miss Pewlish, she almost lost her mind with fear! She kept saying, over and over again, "When is Miss Pewlish coming back? Why has she left us here unsupervised during a school trip?"'

Orlaith's eyes widened with realisation. She jumped to her feet.

'That's right!' she cried. 'She went mad, Miss Pewlish! And she kept threatening to climb into the pen – because . . . because . . .'

Callum stood up. 'Because she thought she'd seen a grown-up in there! I bravely tried to stop her, of course, but in the heat of the moment she slipped into the pen . . .'

'. . . where I mistook the sleeping bear for a chaperone!' Ceri cried. She folded her arms. 'Not that you would have seen any of that, Miss Pewlish – seeing as you were busy buying yourself a cappuccino when it all happened . . .'

'With a hazelnut shot.'

We glanced beside us. Pete had stood up, and leant across the desk at Miss Pewlish.

'*I could smell it.*'

Miss Pewlish fumbled nervously behind her desk, her eyes darting between us.

'You . . . you can't prove anything,' she muttered.

Orlaith blinked innocently. 'Really? We could always check the cameras at the zoo cafe. That is . . . if we *have* to.'

We stood in a line, staring at Miss Pewlish. Her eyes flicked between us. She swallowed dryly. Then, out of nowhere, a beaming smile emerged on her face.

'Well, children,' she said brightly. 'In that case, maybe we should just forget about what happened today. I'm sure it's all just been a *terrible* misunderstanding. Nothing to bother the school safety board with. Don't you agree?'

We all nodded. Miss Pewlish's smile suddenly disappeared, and was replaced with a glare that would blacken stone.

'Now get out of my sight,' she spat.

We scurried towards the door, gazing at each other in dizzy disbelief. We had just achieved the unthinkable. Together, the five of us had fought Miss Pewlish and the Storm Laws, and we had won. We weren't just a bunch of frightened schoolchildren any more.

We were the Tornado Chasers.

9
The First Official Meeting of the Tornado Chasers

I knocked anxiously at the metal door.

'Callum!' I whispered. 'Quick! Let me in!'

There was no answer – at least, nothing I could hear over the groan of the wind behind me, rippling up my jacket. It was growing stronger and stronger every day. I shivered, and glanced over my shoulder across Callum's back garden. There was no sign of anyone through the windows of the enormous square house at the end of the lawn. It was practically a mansion.

The door of the shelter suddenly burst open, and a hand dragged me inside and threw me to the floor. I looked up. Callum slammed the door shut.

'The secret knock, Owen,' he muttered. 'Honestly. How many times did I explain it to you?'

'Oh yeah,' I muttered. 'Sorry.'

I got to my feet, dusting off my shorts, and looked around the shelter. It was a curved iron roof, dug into the ground and held up from inside with a strong timber frame. Along the beams were rows of neat bunk beds. A simple wooden table and chairs stood in the middle of the floor, lit by an electric lamp.

'Wow,' I said. 'I can't believe your parents have their own storm shelter.'

'Yep,' said Callum. 'They're pretty loaded.'

I looked at him. 'What do they do? Why are they so rich?'

Callum ignored me, and focused all his attention on loading a BB gun in his hands. I frowned.

'Er . . . why do you have a gun, Callum?' I said.

He glared at me dramatically. 'Why do you think, Owen? *Protection.*'

I blinked. 'Protection from what?'

Callum rolled his eyes. '*Murderous Pete!* He'll be here with Orlaith any minute. I'm not taking any chances with either of them. If we annoy Orlaith, she'll probably give Pete orders to rip our arms off.'

Knock knock.

Callum paled, and hurriedly handed me the BB gun.

'Keep an eye on them,' he whispered. 'If anything goes wrong, I want you to shoot them both.'

I gawped. 'Me? But I can't . . . !'

Callum had already opened the door before I could finish. I quickly shoved the gun in my pocket as Orlaith stepped inside. She was dressed in a grey skirt and white shirt, both neatly ironed. She looked even smarter than when she was in her school uniform, although the wind had made her hair cover her shoulders and most of her face.

'H-hi Orlaith,' I squeaked, my knees shaking. The gun weighed heavy in my pocket. 'Is, er . . . Pete with you?'

Pete squeezed through the doorway behind her with some difficulty, and stood in the lamplight.

'Hi guys,' he mumbled.

Callum and I both stared at him. Murderous Pete was wearing a baby-blue T-shirt with a picture of a unicorn on it, and matching shorts. He also wore a baseball cap, which also had a picture of a unicorn on it. He held up a Tupperware box and rattled it shyly.

'I made us some fun buns,' he said.

Ceri suddenly burst through the metal door behind him, beaming.

'Sorry I'm late, everyone!' she gasped. 'Woof! That wind, eh? Ooh, are those fun buns?'

Far in the distance, the clock tower chimed for Weekend Curfew to begin. I ran to the shelter door and bolted it shut.

'That's everyone!' I said. 'Quick check – did you all arrange your cover stories for the afternoon?'

The others nodded. We'd all told our parents we were spending the day at each other's houses to practise lines for the school play. Orlaith was at Callum's; Pete was at Orlaith's; Ceri was at Pete's; and I had told my parents I was at Ceri's.

'What about you?' I said, turning to Callum. 'Did you tell your babysitter you were at mine?'

Callum glowered. 'She's *not* my babysi—'

'Great!' I smiled, cutting him off. 'Then I guess . . . this is it. Our first meeting.'

We looked at each other. It was hard to believe that barely a week ago, I hadn't known any of them. And now, together, we were going to do the unthinkable. Orlaith clapped her hands.

'We've got a lot to plan,' she said, 'and not much time to do it. Let's get started.'

Without another word she whipped a sheet from one of the beds and flung it over a beam, weighing down the corners with chairs to make a giant screen. She pulled a marker pen out of her pocket and turned to face us. We were all stood on the spot, staring at her.

'Well?' she muttered. 'Sit down!'

We obediently pulled up chairs around her while Pete distributed the fun buns. Orlaith began drawing on the bed sheet. She moved at lightning speed – in no time at all she had sketched a simple map of the entire village, including the school, the green, the stream, and the road that led out to the valleys, all of it ringed by a giant circle of stormtraps.

'Now, let me get this right,' she said. 'Our plan is to wait until the tornado lands. When it does, we find out when it's due to pass Barrow, then we escape the village, get a photo of us standing next to it and then go home. Correct?'

Everyone nodded eagerly. A fizz of excitement passed through the air.

'Imagine,' I said dreamily. 'The five of us, standing next to a *tornado*.'

'We'd be legends,' said Callum. 'Heroes, even. They'd talk about us for generations.'

'The story of the century,' said Ceri.

We sat in silence for a moment, bathing in the sheer thought. It felt good.

'Well, that's all well and good,' said Orlaith, quickly bursting the bubble. 'But let's face facts. If we're going to go ahead with a plan this risky, then we have to make sure we get it *perfect*. We're going against every Storm Law there is. One wrong step, and all five of us are in serious trouble.'

We glanced at each other. She was right, of course. I got the feeling Orlaith was rarely wrong.

'So how do we do it?' I asked.

Orlaith sighed. 'Well, first of all, we have to get out of the village without being caught. Which means getting past . . . *this*.'

She reached into her bag and pulled out a little figurine. It was a carrot carved into the shape of a man. Orlaith had made him a little yellow outfit out of Post-it notes, and some carefully positioned curly hair from dried seaweed. It was impossible to mistake that mean expression.

'My dad,' said Orlaith, holding up the carrot. 'He patrols the streets each night, *even* when the tornado's landed. And if he catches us, we're going to have to deal with . . . *this*.'

She brought out another carved doll. We gasped. It was a pale white parsnip, with two black olives carefully arranged for glasses, and a black suit made of stitched velvet, and a thin slit for a mouth. It seemed to almost glow in the lamplight. Everyone around me shuddered.

'*The Warden*,' said Callum eerily.

Ceri nodded at the vegetables. 'Nice dolls, by the way.'

Orlaith shrugged. 'I made them at home.'

I put my hand up. 'Er . . . who is this "Warden", exactly? People keep talking about him – why is everyone so afraid of him?'

Callum gave me a withering glare. 'Christ, Owen, he's only the scariest guy in the valleys. How did you not hear about him in Skirting? Did you live in a hole or something?'

Orlaith held the parsnip doll towards me, wiggling it mysteriously.

'He runs the County Detention Centre,' she said. 'That's where they take you if you break the Storm Laws. Most children never come back.'

'Trust us – you don't want to end up there,' said Ceri darkly. 'The Warden is *bad news*.'

I blinked. 'Why?'

There was a long pause.

'They say,' said Pete in a whisper, 'he used to be a bear tracker.'

We all looked at Pete. He had brought his hands up to his mouth, like a giant hamster eating a nut.

'Only the bears . . .' His face suddenly bulged with horror, '. . . *ate his eyes.*'

Orlaith sighed. 'Oh, Pete, come on – that's completely ridiculous.'

'No, it's true!' said Callum, nodding furiously. 'Seriously, I heard he hasn't got any eyes, just big black holes with pus and worms coming out of them and stuff.'

Orlaith groaned. 'Nobody ate his eyes! That's just a stupid story!'

'Then how come he wears glasses all the time, smarty pants?' said Callum. 'Think about it! If he hasn't got any eyes, then he needs glasses to *see.*'

Orlaith put her head in her hands and quietly counted to ten.

'Look,' she said. 'Let's just stick to the facts: if we get caught, then we're going straight to County.' She looked at us gravely. 'And I doubt *anyone* here wants that to happen.'

We took a moment to think about it. I might not have heard much about the Warden, but I certainly didn't want to find out any more.

'So,' said Orlaith, turning back to the bed sheet, 'we'll need to be fast. We need something to get us in and out the village as quickly as possible.'

Callum shrugged. 'Bikes?'

Orlaith rolled her eyes. 'We can't just *cycle* past my dad, Callum.'

'We could if we made them less easy to see,' I piped up. 'You know, like . . .' I fumbled for the right word. '. . . *Stealth* bikes.'

Everyone muttered in agreement.

'God, that sounds cool,' said Callum.

'Yeah!' said Ceri excitedly. 'We could paint them black, so they couldn't be seen in the dark! The helmet, the handlebars, the wheels . . . everything.'

Orlaith thought about it for a moment.

'You know, that could work,' she said. 'I could adapt all your bikes to make them lighter, and faster as well. Put silencers on the wheels, maybe . . .'

'Er,' said Callum. 'Aren't we all forgetting something?'

We looked at him. Callum shifted uncomfortably on his seat.

'Well . . . er . . .' He rubbed at his neck awkwardly. 'There are *certain* members of the gang who might not be able to, you know . . . use a bicycle.' He paused. 'Because of their legs.'

We all turned to look at Ceri. She looked back at us blankly.

'Hmm? What?' she said.

'Er . . . Ceri,' I said carefully. 'Can you use a bike?

With your braces?'

Ceri rolled her eyes. 'What do you think? Of course I can't!'

She turned back to the others.

'But aren't we missing something here? I mean – what's the whole point of us doing this? *To get a photo.* And I'm the best person to do that, aren't I? I'm a photographer! But unless there's someone else riding my bike for me, I'm not going to be able to get a shot – and I'm not going to get off the bike and stand next to a flipping tornado, am I . . . ?'

'Ahem.'

We turned round. Pete had put his hand up, like we were still in school. He looked at us timidly. There was a long pause.

'You can talk, Pete,' Orlaith muttered.

Pete put his hand down. 'My nan's got a special bike. It's got a sidecar – like an old motorbike from black-and-white films.'

'Pete lives with his nan,' Orlaith explained.

Pete nodded shyly. 'It's old, but it still works. My nan would never even notice it's gone. Ceri could sit in it and take photos while I pedal her.'

Orlaith nodded. 'Well then, that's settled. Ceri can share Pete's bike.' She turned to face us. 'Bring them all to the next meeting – back here, same time tomorrow. We can't afford to lose any time – I mean, who knows how long we have left before the tornado lands . . .'

As if on cue, another groan of wind picked up outside, rattling the metal roof. We looked at each other nervously.

'It's coming fast, isn't it?' I said nervously.

'Yeah,' said Ceri with a sigh. 'I hope Flossie's alright.'

I frowned. We all turned to look at her.

'What do you mean, you hope Flossie's alright?' said Orlaith.

Ceri looked at her blankly. 'I mean, I hope she doesn't get blown away or anything. Outside. On the steps.'

She jerked a thumb at the door. We stared back at her in horror. Ceri blinked.

'What?' she said. 'I had to bring her with me, didn't I? She's my Home-Time Partner! Don't worry, she doesn't need a fun bun or anything. I gave her a bag of crisps.'

We all leapt up.

'*You just left her standing outside?*' Callum cried.

Ceri looked confused. 'You . . . you said it was a top-secret meeting.'

'Are you thick?' said Callum. 'It's Weekend Curfew! If anyone sees her standing out there . . . that's it! We're finished!'

Orlaith had already started ripping down the bed sheet.

'Hide the plans!' she cried. 'Owen, quick – run outside and grab Flossie before it's too late! Good grief, she could be halfway across the village by now . . . !'

I stood up. 'Let's not panic. Ceri made a mistake – Flossie's going to be fine. No one's going to be outside today with weather like this anyway.'

I unbolted the door and swung it open.

'She'll probably just be standing in the garden, where no one can . . .'

I turned round, and screamed. Flossie's spit-covered face was hovering barely inches away from my nose. I startled backwards. The others looked up at the door, and gasped.

The shelter was filled with a chilling blast of a valley wind. Slowly, and with great pleasure, Miss Pewlish stepped inside. She gripped Flossie in her hands like a priceless treasure, a hideous grin stretched across her face from ear to ear.

'Well well well,' she said triumphantly. 'Look what I found.'

10

A Storm Approaches

Miss Pewlish looked at each of us with a gloating eye. No one said anything. She placed Flossie on the floor.

'Looking for this?' she said. 'I found her wandering outside, eating some flowers. Not that I *normally* give up my weekends to hide in bushes following the Dewbridge girls, but I thought on this particular weekend I'd make an exception.' She grinned. 'Just in case I found you lot doing, oh I don't know . . . anything you shouldn't.'

Callum suddenly leapt forwards.

'Why, *there* she is!' he said with relief. 'Flossie, you little scamp! We've been looking for her *everywhere*, haven't we guys?' He grabbed Flossie and started strolling out the door. 'Thanks for your help, Victoria.

We'll go back to the house now and . . .'

'SILENCE!'

Miss Pewlish slammed her fists onto the table, her cheeks quivering. Callum flew back. She stared at him with glee.

'Not this time, Brenner!' she hissed. 'Not this time! I'm finally getting rid of you for good. You and all your smart-alec friends!' She turned to Ceri. 'Five children playing unsupervised in a storm shelter during Weekend Curfew, with one Home-Time Partner left outside by herself . . . how many Storm Laws do you think that breaks, Miss Smarty Pants?'

Ceri gulped. 'Loads, probably.'

Miss Pewlish grinned. 'Correct! Enough to get every single one of you a personal meeting with the Warden, that's how many!'

We looked at each other. There was no doubt what was going to happen now. The truth would come out, one way or another. They would find out what we were planning to do. It was all over. Miss Pewlish cackled manically.

'Thought you could get one past "mad old Victoria Pewlish", did you?' she seethed. 'Because she's just a big joke to everyone? Because no one understands her? Because her pioneering vision of a valley-wide child-safety system is "unstable"? Ha! Well then, who's "unstable" now?'

We glanced at each other. None of us had the faintest idea what Miss Pewlish was talking about. It sounded like she was going mad.

'Well, you can't argue your way out of this one!' she shrieked. 'You're going down! You'd need a flipping *miracle* to . . .'

EEEEEEEEEEEEEEEEEEEEEEEEEEEEEEEE
EEEEEEEEEEEEEEEEEEEEEEEEEEEEEEEE

The sound filled the shelter as if from nowhere, high and piercing and distant. Miss Pewlish looked around frantically.

'What is that?' she snapped. 'What's going on?'

EEEEEEEEEEEEEEEEEEEEEEEEEEEEEEEE
EEEEEEEEEEEEEEEEEEEEEEEEEEEEEEEE

The sound rang on, humming through the air and beating off the metal walls. We winced. It seemed almost to wind through the air and burrow into our ears.

EEEEEEEEEEEEEEEEEEEEEEEEEEEEEEEE
EEEEEEEEEEEEEEEEEEEEEEEEEEEEEEEE

Miss Pewlish suddenly looked up, as if stung. Her face slowly drained of colour.

'Oh no,' she said quietly. 'Not now.'

Orlaith suddenly bolted out the door, and without a

word we followed her, across Callum's garden and out into the street. All around us, trees arched and groaned in the breeze, their summer branches trembling and clawing at each other, as if they knew what was coming over the hills.

Across the horizon, each and every stormtrap circling the valley top around Barrow had switched on. Their red bulbs flickered across the hills like bloodspots. The sound of a thousand wailing stormtraps slowly reached us, and grew into a single high-pitched cry that blanketed the village beneath the dark clouds. We looked at each other.

'That siren,' said Orlaith. 'It means . . . it means . . .'

There was a sudden screech of tyres, and we swung round. Officer Reade's car had stopped diagonally across the pavement behind us, the doors open, the engine still running. He leapt out the car and raced towards us.

'*Get inside!*' he barked. '*All of you, right now!*'

Orlaith blinked in disbelief. 'Dad, what . . .'

'*The tornado's coming!*'

The people of Barrow had been rehearsing for this day for ten years. They were running out of their houses around us and hammering boards over the windows, dragging their children screaming down the street. Bags of shopping were dropped and abandoned on the pavement, shattering jars of tomato sauce across the asphalt. The air was thick with the sound of sirens, and the wind, and people shouting, names called, car horns being held down in the distance.

Miss Pewlish suddenly caught up with us, and jumped in front of Orlaith's dad.

'Not so fast!' she cried victoriously. She pointed an accusing finger at us. 'Officer Reade, your timing is perfect. I just found these six children breaking curfew in the most irresponsible and . . .'

'Not now, Victoria,' Officer, Reade said impatiently. 'These children need to get home immediately – the tornado's going to be the other side of that hill by tomorrow night!'

Miss Pewlish's face fell. 'But . . . they've broken the Storm Laws! They need to be . . .'

'No, they don't,' Officer Reade growled. 'And if you try to stop them again, Victoria, I'll arrest you myself!'

Officer Reade spun on his heels and made to walk away. He stopped. Orlaith had reached out and grabbed his sleeve.

'Dad,' she said quietly. 'Are we . . . are we going to be OK?'

Officer Reade glanced down at her for a moment, then turned round.

'Not now, Orlaith,' he muttered.

With that he marched back to his car and sped off down the street. Orlaith stood on the spot, watching him disappear down the road.

Miss Pewlish was still stuck in the position Officer Reade had left her, her mouth opening and closing helplessly. She turned to us as if to say something, but was silenced by a sudden bellow of wind over the hills. Her eyes darted to the sky nervously. She hopped from one foot to the other, then without warning she suddenly bolted down the road, furiously shaking a fist over her shoulder.

'This isn't over!' she cried. 'I'll get you children if it's the last thing I do! The second the tornado's gone – you're *finished*!'

We watched as she disappeared into the hedges, and then there was nothing but us and the wind. The street around us had emptied in seconds. All the curtains had been pulled shut, and all the doors were stormboarded. We looked at each other. Everyone looked shocked. Things had suddenly become very real, very quickly.

'Are we . . . still going ahead with it?' I said.

Callum immediately thrust his hand out between us.

'Course we are!' he said. 'I'm not frightened of a stupid storm. Everyone else is still in . . . right?'

He was trying to look away, but he couldn't hide the fact that the hand he held out was trembling. The rest of us quickly put our hands in, not wanting to be seen as the last. There was only one person who didn't.

We turned to her. She was stood facing away, in the direction her father's car had gone.

'Orlaith?' I said. 'Are you . . .'

'Oh, of course I'm going,' she snapped irritably, batting our hands away. 'Do you mind? I'm trying to think here! The tornado's going to be beside the valley tomorrow night. We have to get everything prepared – and fast.'

She turned to Ceri. 'You – get your camera equipment ready. Bring it to the shelter tomorrow. Pete – get your bike and drop it off outside my workshop. Callum's too, while you're at it.'

Orlaith turned to me.

'Owen – we need bear repellent. Do you have any?'

I nodded feverishly. 'Loads.'

Orlaith smiled. 'Good. We'll need as much as we can carry, or we'll be goners out there.' She turned to Callum. 'Go with Owen and get his bike for him.'

Orlaith exhaled, her eyes dancing brightly.

'We all meet back at the shelter tomorrow night,' she said. 'Six o'clock, when the lights go out. I'll have your bikes ready by then.'

Ceri shuffled nervously. 'And if we . . . don't make it?'

'Then you don't come,' said Callum firmly. 'No exceptions. If anyone wusses out, we go without them.' He flashed us an accusatory look. 'Agreed?'

'Agreed,' we said together.

The streetlights suddenly slammed on around us. We glanced up in shock. Without any of us realising it, the sky above us had filled with black clouds.

11

My New Bedroom

My house didn't look like my house any more. The windows and the door were already covered by rollcages of metal wire, stapled across the front like a mask.

There was no sign of Mum or Dad anywhere. The garage door hung open, and a single light bulb swung inside. My bike stood leant against the wall, rattling in the wind.

'There's my bike,' I said, pointing it out to Callum. 'I'll start bringing the boxes of repellent down to the shelter – my parents could be home any second.'

I walked over to the garage door and silently opened it.

'Really?' said Callum behind me. 'Shouldn't you . . . come with me?'

I stopped, and turned round. Callum stared at me. In the swinging light, he suddenly looked very alone.

'I can't,' I said. 'I have to get the boxes.'

Callum nodded. 'Yeah, well – do it quickly, alright?'

He grabbed the bike, and raced out from the garage and into the street.

The house inside was still, and silent, and dark. Nothing but the moaning of the sirens outside and the wind on the windows.

'Mum?' I called out. 'Dad?'

Silence. There wasn't a moment to lose. I ran into the kitchen, throwing open the laundry cupboard. The boxes of repellent were stacked up in the back – enough for my parents to never notice a few missing . . .

'Looking for something?'

I startled, and swung round. Mum and Dad stood in the unlit kitchen behind me. I could just make out their faces, stony and calm and somehow unreadable in the dark. I shook the twitch out of my neck.

'M-mum!' I said. 'Dad! Er . . . no, I wasn't looking for anything at all . . .'

'Where have you been?' asked Mum.

Her voice was calm, but with a note of panic hidden inside it. She stepped towards me, her arms crossed. I swallowed.

'What do you mean?' I said. 'I've been at Ceri's. I just got ba—'

'We've just come from the Dewbridges',' said Mum. 'They said you were never there in the first place. They said she spent the day at her friend Pete's.'

My stomach dropped. I looked at my parents. I still couldn't see what their faces were doing in the darkness. I suddenly began to feel very uneasy.

'I can explain,' I said, stepping forwards. 'You see . . .'

'Don't lie to us, Owen!' said Dad, his voice suddenly high-pitched. 'We know where you were today!'

My heart froze. 'You . . . you do?'

Dad held a trembling hand to his face. 'You were . . . you were . . .' He could hardly bring himself to say it. 'You were climbing trees again, weren't you? Admit it!'

'After everything we've said!' Mum cried.

The two of them stared at me in the darkness of the kitchen. I looked between them, my heart beating. Outside, the wind whined.

'You're . . . you're right,' I said, shaking my head regretfully. 'I admit it. I was climbing trees. I'm so sorry, Mum and Dad. I'll never do it again, I swe—'

Before I knew it, the two of them had leapt forwards and grabbed my arms and legs, lifting me up into the air. I stared at them in horror.

'Wait . . . what are you doing?' I gasped.

'*Quick!*' Dad wailed desperately. '*Before he tries to climb any more trees!*'

Together they hauled me out of the kitchen and started dragging me up the stairs. I thrashed hopelessly in their grip.

'Stop!' I cried, kicking and heaving. 'Where are you taking me? Stop!'

They flew through my bedroom door and slung me onto the bed. I sat up in disbelief. The bed was surrounded by sandbags and chicken wire. The carpet on the floor had disappeared. So too had the posters, the toys – everything. The windows were boarded up. It was the same miserable bedroom where the next day I would spend my 11th birthday, writing under the bed.

I swung round to face my parents. They stood in the doorway, their eyes wide and mad.

'W-what have you done to my bedroom?' I cried.

'We've made it safe, Owen!' said Dad, wringing his hands. 'There'll be nothing that can hurt you now!'

'There's no chance of you climbing any trees now – not in here!' said Mum.

My stomach dropped. I had never seen either of them look so frightened before. I suddenly understood what Callum was talking about – my parents had gone completely insane. I leapt towards the shutters and tugged at the handles. They rattled hopelessly in my hands.

'That won't work, Owen,' said Mum. 'They're locked from the outside. You don't ever need to be frightened again, angel!'

'It'll just be for a while,' said Dad desperately. 'Just a little while. Until we can be sure you'll be safe. Until *everything's* safe again.'

I leapt to my feet. 'Wait – what do you mean . . . ?'

'We're locking you in your bedroom, darling,' said Mum. 'Until the storm has gone.'

'Until the beginning of the next school year, actually,' said Dad. 'Just to be on the safe side.'

I stared at them in disbelief, and stepped forwards. '*What?*'

'*Quick!*' said Dad. '*Lock the door, before he tries to get out!*'

Mum gripped the door handle and swung it shut. I stumbled desperately over the floorboards but I was too late. The door slammed shut, and the lock turned. I jiggled the foam handle hopelessly.

'Mum! Dad! Please!'

I hammered and hammered against the door, but it was no good. They weren't listening any more.

The wind suddenly picked up outside, pounding

against the house and rattling the shutters like angry ghosts. I pressed myself against the door, my heart pacing with fear. And yet at that moment, what frightened me wasn't the wind, or the dark, or even the realisation that my parents had lost their minds.

It was the thought that my friends had no idea what had just happened. They would wait for me tomorrow night. And when I didn't turn up, they would think I had deserted them. That I had let them down. That I was a coward. And they would leave without me.

And the one chance I had ever had in my life to be a daredevil – to be a real-life Tornado Chaser – would be gone forever.

The last of the clouds covered the sun, and my bedroom was thrown into darkness.

This notepaper is kindly provided for the inmates of
THE COUNTY DETENTION CENTRE
Use one sheet per week
No scribbling

And so, Warden, we come back to where I started. Back to the night we escaped.

By now, you're probably a little confused. Why am I writing my story like this? Why don't I just tell you everything like you asked?

The truth is that I tried to - and I couldn't. Remember back when I said that this was the only way I could tell my story? I really meant it. When I began writing, I had no idea how to get it all out. I started over and over again, hundreds of times. I threw each new attempt away before I even finished the first page, straight out the window of my cell. The pile had become pretty high last time I looked.

This is what I ended up with. It might
not be what you asked for, or what you
wanted, but like I said: it's the only way
I could tell it. For now, you might as well
keep reading.

Who knows - you might even find out
where I've gone!

YOURS SINCERELY,
INMATE 409

12

How it Began, Again

'You. Me. *The Tornado Chasers.*'

Callum stood before me, my bedroom shutters flapping madly in the wind behind him. His trainers were stained green with moss from climbing the tree outside my window. He threw down his samurai sword, and tore off his balaclava, and pointed to the shattered pop-tart at my feet.

'You gonna eat that?' he said.

I shook my head. Callum grinned.

'Get in.'

He scooped the crumbs off the floor and greedily stuffed them into his mouth. He looked around my bedroom, at the bare floor and single light bulb.

'Nice room,' he muttered. 'Love what you've done with it.'

I blushed. 'It was my parents. They got rid of everything.'

'Right,' he said. 'And, er . . . the ham?'

He pointed to the '11' of ham that was stuck to the wallpaper.

'It's my birthday,' I explained.

'Oh,' said Callum.

There was a long pause while Callum finished eating the crumbs from the floor. I stood, staring at him. He looked at me incredulously.

'*What?*' he muttered.

'Callum,' I said. 'What are you doing here?'

He gave me a blank look.

'I told you already – it's six o'clock! We've got a meeting to go to, remember? And here *you* are, eating floor cake and wall pizza like some sort of king . . .'

I stepped forwards.

'But we all agreed yesterday,' I said. 'If anyone didn't show up, the rest of us would just . . . go ahead without them.'

Callum shrugged. 'Yeah, well – I saw your parents arrive just after I took your bike. I figured you might need a little help, seeing as they're so mental.'

I blinked. 'You . . . you came back to get me?'

Callum rolled his eyes.

'Owen,' he said. '*Please*. As *if* I'd let you wuss out now on the most important adventure of our lives! I can't chase a tornado without you.'

I smiled. 'You can't?'

'Course not,' said Callum. 'You're my human shield, remember?'

He gave me a smack on the helmet that was meant to be playful but still hurt quite a lot.

'Thanks,' I said. It wasn't much of a compliment, but it was the best one I'd ever get from him.

'Well, come on then!' he said. 'Let's go before your parents come back and *really* lose it. Grab your stuff and meet me at the bottom of the tree.' He pulled on his balaclava. 'Oh, and, er . . . try not to fall out of it this time.'

He sniggered, and in a flash he had leapt out the window and was gone.

■ ■ ■

Magnolia Crescent had become a ghost town overnight. Cars were left abandoned in the middle of the street, their doors wide open, their windscreens bleached with valley dust. The shopping I had seen thrown to the ground the day before was still there, the plastic bags flapping wildly in the breeze. High above us the stormtraps twinkled on the hilltops, surrounding the valley in a flickering red cage of light. The wind blew slow and steady.

'You ready?' Callum whispered.

'One moment,' I said.

I looked back up to the bedroom shutters I had locked behind me. I could still see a crack of light between them. I held my breath, and waited. Suddenly the light disappeared. I sighed with relief. My parents had turned it off – they thought I was in bed. I was safe to be out until morning.

The two of us crept down the road to Callum's house. It was like we were walking through another version of Barrow, a night version where nothing made sense any more. Garden gates slammed open and shut, and backyard swings strained wildly at their chains and tangled themselves into knots. Flurries of valley dust drifted down the empty roads beside us like great moving monsters. By the time we arrived at Callum's house, the whole street was in darkness. At the end of the garden I could just make out a crack of light peeking under the doorway of the shelter.

'Looks like the others are already there,' I whispered. 'Should I go first, or . . .'

Callum suddenly clamped his hand over my mouth, and flung me into the bushes.

'*Mmmmph . . . !*' I cried.

We hit the ground just as a pair of headlights swung across the lawn where I'd been standing. They slowly panned across the front of the house, casting the squirming bushes around us in a yellow glow. Beneath the roaring wind I could just make out the hum of a car engine.

'*Orlaith's dad,*' Callum hissed into my ear.

The lights stopped and held for a moment. A stream of bitter dust danced through the air. I didn't dare breathe. Then, slowly, the car moved on, and the light faded. The hedges were once again blanketed in darkness. Callum waited until the sound of Officer Reade's car had drifted into silence, and then shoved me away.

'What are you touching me for?' he muttered. 'Weirdo.'

We crept across the back garden. Outside the shelter, all was silent. The bushes rustled menacingly in the wind beside us.

'The door's unlocked,' Callum whispered. 'You go first.'

I smiled. 'Really? Thank you Callum, that's very . . .'

'Just do it,' Callum suddenly snapped, shoving me forwards.

I stumbled through the door and was almost blinded by the brightness inside. I squinted against the hum of light. The shelter was unrecognisable. The beams across the ceiling were lined with candles, lamps and fairy lights, glowing and twinkling like stars. In front of me stood Orlaith, Pete and Ceri. All three were holding presents.

'*Now!*' said Ceri.

Pete quickly pulled on a cord that hung down beside him, and a large banner unfurled from the ceiling. The words 'HAPPY BIRTHDAY OWEN!' were written along it in big bubble letters. Callum strode in and slammed the door behind him.

'Happy birthday, ratbag,' he said. 'Hope you're grateful.'

I stared at the shelter, dumbstruck. 'How . . . how did you . . . ?'

Orlaith stepped forwards. 'Ceri saw your birthday on Miss Pewlish's register. Pretty good timing.' She shoved a shoebox into my hands. 'Happy birthday, Owen.'

I wordlessly opened the box. Inside was a small figurine, carved from a sweet potato. I lifted it out. It was me. It had a mushroom helmet, held on by a single chive chinstrap. Before I could even thank her Pete barrelled forwards and thrust a scarf into my hand.

'Habirday,' he mumbled as he scurried away.

I looked at the scarf. It was handmade, and had tassels at the end. Pete had even knitted my name into the pattern: *OWIN*. Well, it was close enough.

'Thank you, Pete,' I said. 'It's lovely.'

'It's going to be pretty windy,' he muttered, blushing.

'I got you something too!' said Ceri, handing me a package wrapped haphazardly in newspaper. 'Go on, look! Look!'

I pulled aside the crumpled newspaper. There was nothing inside it.

'It's empty,' I said.

'Look at the front!' said Ceri excitedly.

I turned the paper over, and smiled.

SPECIAL BOY TURNS ~~10~~ \\ TODAY!

Local boy Owen bowled over by
personalised newspaper gift.

'It took flipping ages to make, so he'd
better like it,' says our source.

'Best present ever, right?' said Ceri proudly. 'Sorry I got your age wrong. Everything else in the article is accurate though. In fact there are a couple of quotes from Callum you might not be too happy about.'

I beamed at them.

'Thank you,' I said, stepping forwards. 'All of you. This is the best birthday of my . . .'

'*STOP!*' Orlaith screamed, holding out her hand.

I froze mid-step. Orlaith pointed down at the ground. My foot was hovering only inches away from a doormat that had been placed at the entrance. I recognised it immediately – it was the booby-trapped burglar alarm she had made for her presentation. I glanced up. Sure enough, hanging from the ceiling were a series of water rifles aimed directly at my head, filled with stinking month-old mayonnaise.

'For intruders,' Orlaith explained. 'We can't be too careful now my dad's on patrol.' She turned to Callum. 'Any sign of him outside?'

Callum nodded. 'He just passed the house.'

Orlaith sighed, and wiped her face. She looked exhausted.

'Good,' she said. 'That gives us another half-hour at least before he's round here again. Now's our chance, let's go!'

Without another word she strolled over to a tarpaulin sheet that lay at the back of the shelter, and whipped it off with a flourish.

We gasped. In front of us stood our bikes. At least, they *used* to be our bikes. They were more than that now, much more. Orlaith had obviously been working on them all night, taking them to pieces and stripping them down to make them feather-light before welding them back together. The new frames were needle-thin, sleek, already itching to move. Each and every one had been painted midnight black. Orlaith rested a hand on one proudly.

'I didn't get a wink of sleep, but it was worth it,' she sighed, rubbing her eyes. 'They've all got silencers on every moving part, and I've almost halved their weight. Plus, the black paint is a special non-reflective type that doesn't glint in the dark. My dad wouldn't notice us even if we were stood right in front of him.'

'Ooh!' said Ceri. '*Tell* me that one's mine! Please!'

At the end stood the bike with a sidecar. We cooed in amazement. Orlaith had added new panels around the sides to reshape it, all polished to within an inch of their lives. It was like a bullet, beetle-black, moulded to perfection.

'That one took the longest,' said Orlaith proudly, attempting to sound modest and failing. 'All the wheels have got padded suspension now, so you won't get any wobbly photos. Plus, I added a few of my own . . . *adjustments*.'

She patted a metal box on the front of the bike. It had a screen on the front, and a light bulb on top. It made the sidecar look almost like the cockpit of a plane. My eyes widened.

'Hang on,' I said. 'Is that a stormtrap?'

Orlaith stifled a yawn. 'Yep – an old one my dad had lying around. I used it to help me design the stormtrap for the play. But get this – I played around with it last night, and managed to fix the wiring inside.'

She flicked a button at the base of the stormtrap. The bulb on top glowed steadily awake. Orlaith tilted the box towards us.

'Remember what stormtraps do? They push tornadoes *away*. Well, who knows what could happen when we're out there – the tornado could suddenly change direction when we're right next to it, and come towards us. This little box might just save our lives.' She reached into the sidecar. 'And then of course, there's . . . *this*.'

She carefully twisted a hidden mechanism. At once, a specially made tripod flipped up from beside the seat, ready for a camera to be loaded into it. Ceri squirmed with excitement.

127

'Orlaith, you genius!' she said. 'I can't believe you made all this in one night!'

Orlaith shrugged, and pretended to inspect her nails. 'Whatever. It wasn't so hard.'

Callum glared at her jealously. 'Oh, right. Just had all this stuff lying around the house, did you?'

Orlaith bristled. 'An engineer always finds a use for something.'

'*That's* what you want to do when you grow up?' said Callum. 'Be an *engineer?*'

Orlaith blushed. 'It's a well-paid career. With excellent prospects.' She fumbled awkwardly. 'Er . . . shall we?'

We didn't need telling twice. We ran to the bikes and grabbed them eagerly. I almost toppled backwards when I did – my bike had become as light as a feather.

'Wait!' Orlaith cried. 'I almost forgot – there's *one* more thing.'

She reached into the sidecar again and brought a pile of black sheets. She held one up.

'I realised last night,' she said. 'There's no point riding stealth bikes if we're not hidden too, is there?'

She scurried around us, fastening the sheets to our necks and wrists. We looked down at ourselves. Each one of us now wore a lightweight jet-black cape, stretching from our shoulders down to our ankles and hiding our bodies in complete velvet darkness. A face mask attached to the neck, covering our mouths so that only our eyes showed. We looked at each other in the light of the shelter.

'Capes,' said Callum, his voice trembling with barely suppressed excitement 'We look like flipping ninjas!'

'Or superheroes,' said Ceri dreamily. 'A team of superheroes.'

There was no denying it – we looked amazing. Those photographs of my grandparents beside the tornado, in their homemade outfits and specially adapted planes – they were *nothing* compared to this.

'I . . . I don't think I've ever looked this cool in my whole life,' I whispered.

'Which reminds me,' said Orlaith, grabbing another patch of material and chucking it at me. I opened it in confusion.

It was a black shower cap.

'To cover your helmet,' Orlaith explained.

And with that, my moment of coolness passed.

13

Our Daring Escape

A howl echoed down through into the village, carried from far beyond the hills.

'Hear that?' Orlaith whispered. 'That's the tornado. It must be right on the other side of the valley.'

We stood in the bushes, silent, nervous, our eyes darting down the windswept street before us. It was empty. The wind billowed through our lightweight cloaks. My shower cap rustled.

'Remember,' said Orlaith, 'my dad's going to be circling the green by now. So keep your eyes peeled for him. I'll go in front and head for the road out of town – the rest of you follow. Owen, stick at the back and keep an eye out for any bears behind us.'

I nodded. My heart was pounding against my ribcage like a piston. I was surprised the others couldn't hear it over the wind. It rippled through our capes, flapping them out behind us. Orlaith braced herself on her bike.

'*Ready?*' she said.

We pulled on our masks. Orlaith gave us one last glance. A smile winked at the corner of her eyes.

'*The Tornado Chasers!*' she hissed.

And with that she was off, whipping out the bushes at lightning speed and disappearing round the corner. Callum leapt up and down on his bike in excitement.

'The Tornado Chasers!' he said.

Without another word he kicked his bike away and shot after her. Ceri stood up in the sidecar and held out her cape to the wind.

'The Tornado Chasers!'

Pete grinned and heaved himself down onto the pedals. They powered out of the bushes and flew down the street, Ceri giggling with excitement and slapping Pete on the bum to make him go faster.

I watched them disappear, and waited for a second. I quickly glanced over my shoulder. I could *swear* I heard something rustling in the bushes behind me. I swallowed, and pushed myself off.

'The Tornado Cha . . .' I managed.

I flew out the bushes like a rocket, swerving wildly into the empty street and almost toppling over. I gasped. Orlaith had completely transformed my bike – it was like riding on a cloud. The speed was unbelievable. With every stroke I surged forwards, cutting through the wind like a razorblade, the wheels responding to even the slightest movements of my body. I'd never felt anything like it. All of a sudden I found myself standing upright on the pedals, as high as I could manage, the cape fluttering ghost-silent round my shoulders.

'A *daredevil*,' I cried, almost a laugh. 'I'm doing it. I'm doing it!'

Up ahead, the others flickered in and out the streetlights like moths, through the sleeping village streets, past the broken and boarded-up houses that lined the empty roads of Barrow. I glanced at the rows of identical houses, at the people hidden inside, and almost felt sorry for them. They had no idea how this felt – to be outside, riding bikes in the wind, with no one to know but us. *To chase a tornado*. I felt more terrified, and more free, than I had ever felt in my entire life.

We slipped across the green and down the road that led out into the valley. There were no streetlamps here, and we cycled in pitch black, threading the bikes against the wind that flooded into the valley. The hills lay ahead, a black wall stretching across the landscape. The red lights of the distant stormtraps glimmered in a row on top of them. Above them the night sky was moonless and thick with dust. Somewhere out there was the tornado, heading towards the village.

The others came to a stop up ahead. I gripped on the brakes, and pulled up beside them.

A roadblock lay ahead. I recognised it immediately – my parents and I had driven through it when we first arrived at Barrow. It was a small guard's hut, with a thick metal barrier that stretched from one end of the road to the other, painted bright red and surrounded by warning signs. It had taken two guards to lift the barrier from its stand and let us through. Now, of course, the guard's hut was empty. The sign behind it creaked and swung in the wind.

YOU ARE NOW LEAVING BARROW:
THE SAFEST VILLAGE IN THE VALLEYS.

!!!WARNING!!!

IMMEDIATE DANGER OF BEARS AND
TORNADOES AHEAD.

INCREASED LIKELIHOOD OF SUDDEN,
TERRIBLE DEATH.

ANY CHILDREN WHO STEP BEYOND
THIS POINT WILL BE SENT STRAIGHT
TO THE COUNTY DETENTION CENTRE
IF THEY MAKE IT BACK ALIVE.

Orlaith turned to face us, her eyes glimmering fiercely
above her mask.

'Where we stand now,' she said, 'is the last point
before we violate the most serious Storm Law in Barrow.
Leaving the village.' She looked at us. 'Are we all still
in?'

We nodded quickly, as if we didn't want to think too
much about it. The wind howled down the valleyside
towards us. The tornado was getting closer.

'Right,' said Orlaith. 'Well, let's just get it over with,
then.' She turned to the metal barrier. 'I guess we'll
have to find a way of lifting this up first . . .'

Pete calmly stepped forwards, and with the slightest
of grunts took the great metal barrier in his hands and
lifted it off the stand. We all oohed in admiration. Pete
turned back round with a sheepish grin, holding the

barrier in his arms like it was a nice pet rabbit.

'Thanks Pete,' said Orlaith. 'Right, let's get out of here before my dad—'

She suddenly stopped, and swung round.

'My dad!' she gasped. 'Wait – did anyone see him?'

Her voice was tight with panic. We looked at each other blankly. There had been no sign of him at the green.

'That doesn't make any sense,' said Orlaith, confused. 'We *should* have seen him . . .'

We glanced at each other nervously.

'Maybe he went a different way round?' suggested Ceri.

Orlaith frowned. 'Like where? It's a tiny village!'

I shrugged. 'Maybe he took a back road on the way round, and we missed him?'

Orlaith shook her head. 'Then . . . where would he be now?'

A pair of headlights suddenly appeared behind me.

I swung round. There, flying towards me and getting closer every second, was Officer Reade's car. Before I could even think of moving, I startled. My whole body froze from top to bottom. I realised there and then that the car was going to hit me – all I could do was watch it happen. It was over in seconds. I saw Officer Reade's eyes widen and his foot slam down, and heard the screech of his brakes, and –

WHAM.

I was flung backwards through the air, and landed hard on the cold earth that lay beside the road. The breath was slammed out of me, and as I swung back my helmet came down against the tarmac with a sickening *crack*.

For a while – or what seemed like a while – all I could do was lie still and make out the different sounds around me. My heartbeat. The wind howling across the fields. A car door slamming.

'Oh no!'

And then suddenly the adrenaline rushed through me and I gasped in a freezing clutch of air. My ribcage swelled and deflated against the ground, and my brain reeled. *I had just been hit by a car.* And something about my head felt wrong – very wrong.

I pushed myself up, and looked down. There were things on the ground around me where I had landed. Lots of things. I reached out and picked one up.

It was a shard of plastic.

'My helmet,' I muttered.

I touched the top of my head. There, instead of smooth plastic, I felt a set of jagged edges where the helmet had shattered apart. My head underneath was completely unharmed. A hand suddenly grabbed me and flipped me onto my back. Officer Reade looked down at me, bent over in the sickly glow of the headlights. He looked terrified.

'Oh, thank God,' he gasped, his face flooding with relief. 'Thank God! I thought you were . . .'

He suddenly stopped, and heaved me to my feet. The hardness came back to his face in an instant.

'Are you *insane?*' he cried. 'What the *hell* are you doing out here? I could have killed you, you . . . you *idiot!*'

He flipped round to the others. They stood frozen to the spot. Pete was still holding the barrier in his arms, trembling from head to toe.

'*What is this?*' he shouted. 'The tornado's the other side of the hill, and you're all standing in the street, in the middle of the night – dressed up like flipping *Batman?*'

His whole body had clenched with anger. The others stared at him, their terrified eyes the only part of their face visible above the masks.

'*Get in the car!*' he screamed. 'And take those stupid costumes off! When I find out who you are, you're all in *serious* trouble!' He pointed a finger at Pete. 'And as for you – put that barrier back, *right now!*'

Pete squeaked in terror, and swung round.

CLANG.

The next thing I knew, Officer Reade was slumped onto the tarmac beside me.

The four of us looked at his motionless body in horror. Pete stopped, and turned back round. He looked at us, then at Officer Reade, then at the barrier in his hands. He took a moment to work out what had happened, before crying out and dropping the metal pole on the ground like it was burning red hot. Orlaith suddenly ran forwards and knelt beside her father.

'Dad! Dad! Are you OK?'

'Uuurgh . . .' Officer Reade gurgled.

She turned him onto his back. He had been knocked out cold. On top of his head was now a small, straight cut where the barrier had hit him, an angry lump forming rapidly around it.

'Oh no,' said Orlaith. 'Oh no, oh no, oh no . . .'

The radio in the car let out a sudden burst of feedback.

'*Officer Reade*,' came a loud, crackly voice. '*Come in, Reade – we need an update of your location, please.*'

Callum's eyes widened.

'What do we do?' he said, desperately. 'What do we do?'

None of us said anything. We didn't even move. Our gaze was fixed on the Barrow Truancy Officer that we had just knocked unconscious. We tried to work out how we could explain what had happened. To work out how much trouble we were in now. To think if there was any way of fixing it, of turning back time, of undoing what had been done.

'Reade,' repeated the voice on the radio. 'Come in, Reade.'

Officer Reade's eyes suddenly blinked open. 'Orlaith? Is that you, Orlaith?'

We looked at each other. Of course, we *knew* there was no way of undoing it. It was too late for that now. There was only one thing left we *could* do.

'Reade?'

The five of us turned and leapt onto our bikes, and without a word we flew through the open barrier and up the hillside, away from the village and the terrible mess we had made, charging towards the tornado as fast as we could.

14

The County Officers

By the time we finally came to a stop, Barrow was far behind us. We had no idea how long we'd been cycling for. The forest around us was alive with wind. Tree trunks groaned and their branches flailed, fighting against the gale that blew mercilessly down the hill. The tornado was close now. Very close.

Not that we could get to it.

Ahead of us lay a tree cutting off the only road out of Barrow. It cut off both lanes, blocking a stream on one side and a sodden ditch on the other. The trunk was at least three times our height. There was no way any of us could get around it.

Callum was the first to stop cycling. He took his feet

off the pedals and rested his shaky legs on the tarmac, before immediately toppling over and sprawling across the ground like a slug. I quickly followed his example, twitching uncontrollably on the tarmac. Pete slumped his bike sideways and sent Ceri tumbling across the road. Orlaith fell to the floor and wrapped her cape around her head in misery.

'Oh Pete,' she groaned. 'What were you *thinking*?'

Pete lay on his back, heaving for breath. 'I . . . I didn't mean to . . .'

He was cut off by terrible roar of wind above us. We looked at each other. It was as if the tornado was laughing at us, at what we had tried to do, at all our failed plans. I pulled my helmet slowly off my head. It was shattered, broken beyond repair.

'This is so bad,' I whimpered.

'It's worse than *bad*!' said Ceri, sitting up. 'We just knocked out a *Truancy Officer*!'

Callum sat up to face her.

'We?' he snarled. '*WE!* I don't seem to remember trying to murder anyone with a ten-foot metal pole!' He pointed at Pete. 'It was all him! That . . . that *psycho*!'

Pete flinched, and then sat still. No one said anything. After a while he got to his feet, and walked silently down the road. Orlaith leapt up.

'Pete, wait!' she cried. 'Where are you going? Come back!'

Callum snorted. 'Let him go! Who knows – maybe he'll do us all a favour and disappear into the woods forever . . .'

Orlaith glowered at him. 'Leave him alone! It was an accident!'

Callum slapped his cheeks in mock surprise. 'Oh, of course! It was an accident! *Murderous Pete* didn't mean to brain your dad at all! What a terrible misunderstanding!'

Orlaith seethed with fury. *'Don't call him that, Callum!'*

Callum stamped his feet angrily. *'I'll call him whatever I . . .'*

He was stopped by a sudden loud *splash* behind us, quickly followed by another. We swung round. Pete was striding up the road towards us, water pouring from his sodden cape. We silently watched as he lifted both his bike and mine onto his shoulders, before strolling back to the riverbank with them as easily as if he was carrying a pair of feathery pillows. He threw them into the water. In the stream I could just make out the handlebars of our other two bicycles.

'Er . . . Pete?' said Orlaith. 'Pete, what are you doing?'

Pete didn't respond. He marched up the hill towards us, his eyes hardened with the look of a man who knows what he has to do. In a matter of seconds he had lifted me straight off the ground and wedged me under his arm, before striding up to Callum and doing the same. I tried to struggle free, but it was no use – Pete had the strength of a horse. He marched us straight over to the ditch that ran alongside the road and flung us down into the weeds and the muck and the slime.

I emerged, gasping for breath. The water at the bottom was shallow but freezing cold, and the mud lay thick underfoot. In front of me Callum was almost delirious with fear, thrashing about and covered from head to toe in brown sludge.

'Oh God, I knew it!' he cried. 'It's finally happening! He's going to murder us! Orlaith, stop him!'

There was a muffled yell from the roadside above, and a second later Orlaith and Ceri landed with an almighty *splash* in the ditch beside us. Orlaith looked up at the roadside, her eyes wide with confusion.

'Pete – what are you doing?' she cried. 'Stop! *Don't!*'

Without warning Pete came crashing down beside

us, hitting the sludge like a ship being launched and covering us with a wall of stinking bilge water. We coughed and spluttered, flinging pond scum out of our eyes with both hands. Pete was crouched down low in the water, so that only his childlike eyes lay blinking and terrified above the sludge.

And then we heard it – a car.

We swung round. There, driving up the road towards where we had just stood, was a black van. On the side, in white letters, read the words: COUNTY DETENTION CENTRE.

We sunk down into the filthy water beside Pete, as low as we could bear. The sound of the engine grew louder and louder until it came to a stop on the road beside us. Then came the sound of car doors opening, footsteps on asphalt.

'Any sign of them?'

The first voice was deep, tired and irritable.

'Nothing,' said another voice, sharp and nasal. 'I told you – they're all hiding back in the village, no doubt about it.'

'Humph. Pity,' muttered the first one. 'I'd have happily dragged every single one of them back by their ears myself! I mean, honestly – making us go outside in the middle of a bleeding storm . . .'

We held our breaths, blood thundering in our ears.

Please leave, I silently begged. *Please, leave*.

But the men above us were taking their time. One of them whistled appreciatively.

'Well, they won't have gone any further than *that*,' said the second voice, giving the fallen tree trunk a hefty kick. 'If you ask me, they never even left the village in the first place.'

'Too right,' muttered the first voice. 'I'm telling you – she made the whole thing up.'

We glanced at each other. *She?*

'What was it she said again?' said the second voice. '"*Tornado Chasers*", wasn't it?'

The first voice groaned. 'Right, get this – she comes running into County a few hours ago, covered in mayonnaise . . .'

'*Mayonnaise?*' said the second voice.

'Mayonnaise,' repeated the first voice bluntly. 'Mayonnaise from head to toe. And not just *any* mayonnaise – manky, snot-coloured, curdling old mayonnaise. *Months* it's going to take me to get the smell out of my office. Months.'

'What the hell is she doing, leaving the valley and coming to County in the middle of the night?' the second one cried in disbelief.

'That's what I said!' the first one continued. 'But she was beside herself – kept saying five kids from her class were trying to escape the village! Said she'd seen them leave Brenner's storm shelter when she was hiding outside in the bushes. They even made special bikes, she said, and . . .'

'Hang on,' said the second one, cutting him off. 'She was hiding in the *bushes*?'

'Let's just say it's not the first time,' muttered the first one.

Down in the ditch, we glanced at each other. There was no doubt who they were talking about.

'I mean, honestly, she sounded completely demented,' the first voice continued. 'I was going to arrest her for time-wasting right there and then – again! – but then we had a call from Reade. Looks like some kids had knocked him out while he was on patrol. So there we go – looks like there *was* some truth in what the daft old bat was on about!'

The second voice huffed. 'Five children escaping the village? Bunch of kids sneaking out for fun during curfew, more like it. Making up a load of far-fetched stories about how they were going to chase a storm, end up getting caught by Reade and panicking. They'll all be hiding at home, crying their eyes out – mark my words.' He sniggered. 'That is, unless the bears got them first – right?'

The two men suddenly burst into loud and raucous laughter, as if they were sharing a joke that we weren't invited to understand.

'Ha! You're right,' said the first one. 'Let's head back. Leaving the village to chase a tornado . . . I mean, *honestly*. No one's *that* stupid.'

The second one snorted. 'Well, they couldn't do much chasing now. The tornado passed Barrow half an hour ago!'

The two men laughed again, and with a slam of car doors and the rev of an engine they disappeared into the distance, until the van was finally lost to the wind.

We waited a long time until any of us felt ready to move. We stood up, our faces stained brown, our capes heavy with mud. Only Pete stayed crouched in the water. Orlaith reached out to touch his shoulder, but he flinched away. She looked at him pleadingly.

'Pete,' she said. 'Pete, I never thought that you were *actually* going to . . .'

'Yes, Orlaith,' he said, looking up at her. 'You did.'

He stood up to face us. His eyes looked down on us, calm and hurt.

147

'Do you know *why* everyone calls me Murderous Pete?' he said.

We stood, shocked into silence. I had never heard Pete talk like that – it looked like none of the others had either.

'They say I killed my parents,' he said. 'And that's why they're not around any more. Why I just live with my nan.' His eyes suddenly changed – a flash of anger inside them. 'That's what you lot think too – right?'

Silence. Pete looked down.

'They left me with my nan,' he muttered. 'Both of them. When I was a baby. They couldn't look after me, they said. I've never even *seen* them, except in photographs.' He picked at a piece of thread sticking out from his pocket. 'I'm not a murderer.'

No one said anything for a while. Pete stood, his gaze fixed down, his fingertips skimming the surface of the water. Orlaith shook her head.

'Pete,' she said. 'I never knew.'

He shrugged. 'You never asked.'

We glanced at each other. None of us felt very brave any more.

'Sorry, Pete,' I said.

Everyone muttered a guilty apology. Pete looked up at us. His lip was trembling.

'I didn't mean to scare you,' he said. 'I heard the van coming and I thought, if they saw the bikes . . .' His voice broke, just slightly. 'And I'm really sorry about your dad, Orlaith, I never . . .'

Orlaith reached out and touched his shoulder.

'It's fine, Pete,' said Orlaith. 'It's all fine.'

We climbed up the sides of the ditch and stood in the road, assessing the situation. The bikes lay in a tangled heap in the stream. Ceri's camera jutted out the water, dangling by its strap from the tripod. It was a miracle the County officers hadn't seen them.

'How did they get here so *fast?*' said Ceri. 'I mean, I thought the Detention Centre was miles away – and this is the only road out of town, isn't it? How could they . . .'

She trailed off. Nothing made much sense any longer. The storm was gone. Our whole plan had unravelled in front of us. Orlaith sighed, and pulled off her cape.

'Well, I suppose that's it then.'

We fell silent.

'Oh God,' I said, my stomach turning tombstone-cold. 'My parents are going to kill me.'

'We're going to prison,' Pete whispered.

'I'll never see a tornado,' said Callum.

Orlaith squeezed the ditchwater from her cape. 'And I'm never getting into the Valley Academy as long as I live.'

The wind ran through the trees again, scattering the roadside with dead branches. We started at them glumly.

'On the plus side,' said Ceri. 'I suppose it can't get any worse, can it?'

We turned to look at her. She was stood beside the fallen tree trunk, twiddling her cape in her fingers absent-mindedly.

'I mean . . . why not just keep going? Finish what we started? Leave the valley, chase the tornado . . .'

Orlaith frowned. 'Because between us we've already broken about a hundred Storm Laws.'

'A hundred and seven,' Ceri corrected. 'So let's face it – we're going to get locked up whether we go back now or whether they catch us in a few days. By then, a couple of extra months in County won't make any difference. But coming back to the village as heroes – as *Tornado Chasers* – well, that's got to be worth *something*, right?'

We looked at each other. Maybe some blood had pooled in my brain after the car hit me, but Ceri was beginning to make sense. She put her hands on her hips.

'Think about it – Would Owen's grandparents have given up at the first hurdle?' she asked. 'No! They'd have kept going. And I don't know about you, but I didn't join the Tornado Chasers to be cautious and safe and sensible. I joined so I could see *this*.'

She held out her hands. The trees around us had bent double in the roaring wind, their leaves stripped and trembling. The moon and sun both hung above us in the morning light, casting impossible shadows across a forest streaked in whites and blues. It looked like the end of the world. Ceri shook her head.

'I've never seen *anything* like this before,' she said. 'And you know why? Because we spend all our time stuck indoors, *that's* why! Home, school, home, school . . . that's it! And even then, all we ever get told is how we're not being safe enough. I'm flipping sick of it. Aren't you?'

No one said anything. Without another word, Ceri stuck out one of her braces and drew her leg across the tarmac, carving a line between her and us. She stood defiantly on the other side.

'You lot go home if you want to,' said Ceri. She drew her cape about her with a flourish. '*I'm* going to chase a tornado.'

I made to speak, but before I could say anything

Callum had already shoved me aside and marched across the line.

'Yeah, obviously!' he said. 'That's exactly what I was about to say, Ceri. We should definitely just keep going. Glad you agree with me.'

He stood beside Ceri. Orlaith shook her head and made to say something, but trailed off. Pete had stepped forwards. We watched in silence as he slowly crossed the line on the tarmac and stood beside the others. Callum grinned, and slapped him on the back.

'Great!' he said. 'That makes three against two. What about you, Owen? Are you with us?'

I looked at my three friends standing on the other side of the divide. I thought about what my cell in County would look like.

And then I thought about my new bedroom waiting for me back home.

With a sigh, I dropped my broken helmet to the ground. It clattered across the tarmac and rolled into the ditch.

'Well, I'm a Tornado Chaser,' I said. '*Obviously.*'

The others cheered, and patted me on the back. We turned to Orlaith. She stood alone on the road behind us, her eyes pained behind the mask of mud and hair, wringing the cape in her hands. I suddenly noticed how chewed and bitten her nails were.

'Guys,' she said. 'Don't you get it? The tornado's *gone*. The bikes are underwater. Ceri's camera is probably broken. There's a tree blocking the only road out of town.' She shook her head. 'You . . . you can't do it.'

I rolled my eyes. 'Well, of course *we* can't do it, Orlaith. Look at us.'

I nodded encouragingly at the others. We tried to look as pathetic and bedraggled as possible, which was not very hard. Pete had frogspawn in his hair.

'We'd never have got this far without you,' I said pleadingly. 'If you leave . . . we don't stand a chance.'

Orlaith looked us over, her eyes calculating it all. Her fingernails twisted and worked at the cape.

'*Please*, Orlaith.'

She let out a very long, and very deep, sigh. Then with a flourish she lifted up the cape and slung it across her back.

'Fine,' she grumbled. 'Have it your way.'

She marched over the line. Everyone cheered and leapt on top of her, shaking her and ruffling her hair. Orlaith allowed herself a smile for a moment, and then quickly pushed us away.

'Alright, alright! That's enough,' she said. 'Let's get

153

going. They're going to work out we're not in Barrow any moment.'

She pointed to Pete and Callum.

'You two get the bikes out the river. Ceri, check over your camera equipment and make sure it all works. And then . . . well, then still have to get over this flipping tree trunk, don't we?'

She turned to me with a sigh.

'You don't know anything about climbing trees, do you Owen?'

I smiled.

15

The Valleys

We stood on highest point of the hills surrounding Barrow. It had taken all morning to get over the tree and up the hill, pushing the bikes by hand when the road was too steep. The village was barely a speck behind us now. Not that we were looking at it.

The valleys stretched out before us. They rolled on great waves into the horizon, dipping and swelling further than the eye could see. Small villages and towns lay pocketed between the hills, the air above them rippling with chimney smoke and flocks of slow-moving birds. The countryside in-between was spread and shaped by hills and mountains, forests and fields, rivers and eddies and clusters of coloured rock.

'*Told* you it'd be good,' said Ceri.

She was right. It was beautiful. It was probably the most beautiful thing I'd ever seen.

'I've never seen so many stormtraps,' I muttered.

The blinking metal boxes stretched out in both directions beside us, running like a long great chain fence all along the hills. But they didn't just surround Barrow: they ran across the entirety of the valleys, splitting into different pathways and flickering on the top of even the furthest mountains. They seemed almost to form a shape of their own on the landscape.

'The stormtraps surround the valleys like a fence,' Orlaith explained. 'So the tornadoes can't escape. Most of the villages just have one in the middle, though. See?'

She pointed a few of them out. In every village we could just make out a single blinking light in the centre, stuck to the top of the highest building.

'What about that one?' said Ceri, pointing behind us. 'Over there. That doesn't look like a village.'

We turned round and shielded our eyes. In the centre of the valley directly next to Barrow lay a single grey building, surrounded by high walls. It stood alone in a valley filled with rubbish. A single stormtrap blinked on the roof.

'I didn't know there was a valley next to Barrow,' I said, confused. 'It – it looks like . . .'

'The County Detention Centre,' said Orlaith quietly.

A chill suddenly fell on our group.

'*That's* where it is?' said Callum. 'Right next to the village?'

Ceri shuddered. 'Probably so they can catch you quickly if you try to escape.'

We looked nervously at the building. It had all the features of a breeze block. It looked very dark inside. I imagined what it would be like to spend my summer there.

'Well – come on then!' said Callum boldly, breaking the silence. 'No point standing here like a bunch of losers. Let's go get this tornado!'

He pointed to the horizon. High above the hills in the far distance, the sky was stained by a colossal bank of grey clouds. They hovered in the air like a fairytale castle, casting a great shadow onto the slopes below. There was no doubting what it was.

'It looks, er . . . pretty far away,' I said.

Orlaith sighed. 'Well, it's had all morning to get ahead of us, hasn't it? We'll never catch up with it now. If we want another chance to get near it, we're going to need a new strategy.'

I blinked. 'Like what?'

Orlaith's eyes flickered slightly.

'Well, I don't know, Owen,' she snapped. 'I didn't

have time to make an ideas machine last night. Just the bikes. And the stormtrap. Oh, and the capes.' She crossed her arms huffily. 'So maybe someone *else* should come up with the ideas for once.'

We glanced at each other. Orlaith needed careful handling.

'What about the stormtrap?' I asked. 'Could that help us?'

Orlaith groaned. 'Who knows? I mean, it's got some kind of screen on it, but I just can't work out what it's supposed to be showing . . .'

She plucked it from the sidecar and held it up. The screen was filled with a series of dots, laid out across a grid. At the bottom, a single light flashed on and off.

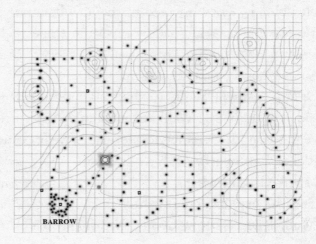

'Looks like a bear,' I muttered.

'Yeah!' said Ceri. 'Or an old bugtrap filled with flies.'

'Or a pile of sick,' said Callum.

Orlaith ran her fingers around the dots in a swirling pattern. 'I've looked and looked at it, but I just can't work out what it's supposed to be . . .'

I frowned, and traced the shape with my eyes. It almost reminded me of something . . .

And then it struck me, as if a light had been switched on in my head. I grabbed the stormtrap from Orlaith's hands and held it up in front of me.

'Hey!' she cried.

I looked between the swirling dots and the valleys, the dipping hills and the lights on the screen, a smile slowly breaking out across my face.

'That's it!' I said. 'That's *it*!'

The others looked at me, nonplussed. I pointed back to the stormtrap excitedly.

'Don't you see?' I said. 'The screen – it's a map of the valleys! All these dots are stormtraps!'

Ceri glanced at me suspiciously. 'How do you know?'

'Well,' I said, 'Barrow's the only village that's surrounded by stormtraps, right?' I ran my finger around the ring of dots in the bottom left corner of the screen. 'That would make it *this* circle here. The dot in the middle must be the one on the clock tower.' I pointed to another dot outside the ring. 'And this one would be the County Detention Centre.'

Orlaith gasped. 'He's right! Owen – you brilliant, brilliant man!'

She ran forwards. I thought she was going to hug me, but she just grabbed the stormtrap out of my hands and turned away. She took a marker pen out of her pocket, pulling off the lid with her teeth. Callum looked at her incredulously.

'You, er . . . always keep a marker pen in your pocket?' he said.

Orlaith ignored him. She set to work doodling across the screen, glancing up across the valleys every few seconds.

'Uh huh . . . so if we're *here*, that would make *that* one Skirting . . . uh huh . . . which would make all *those* the factories in the East . . . and all this up here would be the North . . . There!'

She popped back the lid on the pen and held up the stormtrap. The screen was now covered in pen lines.

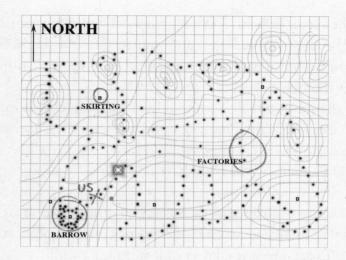

'And that's not even the best bit,' she said, her voice betraying a flicker of excitement. She pointed at the bottom of the screen. 'See that little flashing light just there?'

We looked at the blinking light on the screen, and nodded.

'Look at where the tornado is.'

We turned to the shadow of clouds in the distance, hidden by the hills. They slowly moved across the countryside, further and further out of view.

'It's moving East, right?' said Orlaith. 'Now, look at what the flashing light does.'

We stared at the screen in silence. Orlaith held her

161

thumb to the light. A minute passed. Then, it happened. The light beside her thumb turned off, and the next one along started blinking instead. Orlaith looked up in triumph.

'It shows which stormtrap the tornado is closest to!' she cried. 'Which means . . . *we can work out where it's going to go!*'

We stared at her blankly.

'How?' asked Ceri.

Orlaith moaned with frustration and tugged at her hair. I finally understood why it stuck out so much.

'Don't *any* of you know how stormtraps work?'

Our silence spoke volumes. Orlaith muttered something under her breath about doing everything herself, and held up the stormtrap.

'Right,' she said. 'Stormtraps push tornadoes away. OK? But they don't just push them anywhere – they all work together. That's why they're in a big chain around the whole valley.'

She pointed to the enormous system of stormtraps that wrapped and crisscrossed the valleys around us.

'When a stormtrap senses a tornado is near, it pushes it along to the next one in the chain. Which pushes it along to the next one, then the next one and the next, until the tornado gets pushed all the way to the North.'

She pointed to the horizon, where a range of white mountains dominated the landscape.

'There are no villages or anything there,' she said. 'Just hills and caves. Nothing the tornado can damage.' She struck the stormtrap triumphantly. 'So all we have to do is work out the path the tornado's going to take, and cut it off before it gets there!'

She started scribbling on the display again. The pen raced across the screen, drawing lines, dots, scribbles, everything at lightning pace. She held up the display.

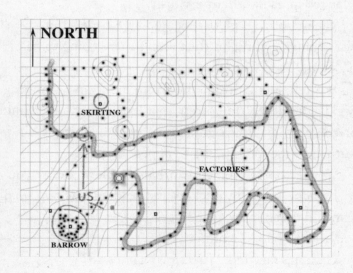

'We'll head right there – the hills below Skirting.' She grinned. 'By the time the tornado's been all around the valleys and is heading back West, we'll be ready and waiting for it.'

We glanced at each other in excitement, our hearts racing. The plan was back on track – we could do this.

'So – how long have we got to get there?' I said.

Orlaith's eyes flicked around the screen. 'Two days, I reckon. Which means . . . well, it means we're going to have to find somewhere to sleep rough for tonight.'

Her words had an immediate effect on the group. We glanced at each other nervously.

'Sleep rough?' Ceri repeated. 'Outside? But . . . if we're outside at night, then aren't there going to be . . .'

'*Bears?*' said Callum nervously.

We fell silent. In all the excitement and planning, we'd completely forgotten that our adventure would involve us cycling right across bear country. Callum turned to me, pretending to appear casual.

'You, er . . . did remember that repellent, didn't you?'

I reached into my pockets and held out the two small cans I'd taken from my bedroom.

'It's all I had,' I whimpered.

Callum's face fell. '*Two* cans? That's all?'

There was an awkward pause. I glanced at Orlaith.

'We should be fine if we find shelter . . .' I said. 'Right, Orlaith?'

Orlaith nodded quickly. 'Yeah – probably. Let's just get moving before it gets dark.'

'Yeah,' said Pete, climbing onto his bike. 'We've only got a few hours before curfew starts, anyway.'

Orlaith stopped suddenly. She turned to him, and smiled.

'Pete,' she said. 'No, we don't. There *is* no curfew. Not out here.'

He looked at Orlaith for a moment. Then, a smile slowly flickered at the corner of his lips.

'Oh, yeah,' he said.

A gust of wind suddenly belted through the grass, scattering pollen in a cloud around us. We gazed at the countryside ahead. It spread out for miles. There were patches of forest, sheep fields, rivers, mountains jutting out the earth and ringed with wisps of cloud. The whole world lay before us. And it was ours.

'No curfews,' said Orlaith. 'No Home-Time Partners. No Storm Laws.'

'We can do anything we want,' I said quietly. 'Go anywhere.'

Ceri grinned. 'So where do you want to go?'

Callum barrelled forwards, his eyes wide with excitement.

'*The forest!*'

He pointed to the other side of the valley. Ahead of us a dense woodland sprouted across the valley floor and up the hills, the layers of branches shimmering in the wind.

'*An actual forest*,' he said. 'Like in books! You know what that means, right? Campfires! Berries on every tree!'

We glanced at each other, breathless with excitement.

'I've never been in a forest before!' I said eagerly. 'I mean, I've been *near* one. But my parents would only let me look at it through binoculars.'

'Me neither,' said Orlaith. 'In fact . . . has *anyone* been camping before?'

Everyone shook their heads. There was no chance any of our parents would have ever let us do something as reckless as sleep outside. Callum snorted.

'Who cares! We've come this far already, right? *We can do this!*' He looked at us, his eyes glimmering. 'By tonight, we'll be bathing in waterfalls, sleeping in treehouse palaces, eating roasted warthog . . .'

Our stomachs groaned the moment he said it. Not one of us had eaten since the day before.

'Oh man,' Ceri groaned, clutching her stomach. 'I could really do with some roasted warthog.'

'Me too,' I said desperately. 'Do you reckon there'll be enough warthog to go around, Callum?'

'Er . . . I dunno, probably,' said Callum. 'I mean, even if there's not *that* much warthog, we'll be OK for a while. Don't you only need to eat, like, once a year or something?'

16

It Turns Out You Need to Eat More Than Once a Year

It was the next day. We stood in a limestone quarry the other side of the valley. It was raining heavily. It hadn't stopped raining for twelve hours. We were looking at a sheep. The sheep was looking back at us.

'Somebody kill it already,' said Callum, his voice breaking.

Nobody moved. Callum pushed me forwards.

'Owen, kill the sheep,' he said.

I looked at the sheep. The sheep chewed thoughtfully on something.

'What if it bites me?' I said nervously.

'I'll bite you if you don't bleeding kill it,' snapped

Callum. 'Forget it! You're useless. Pete, kill the sheep.'

Pete whimpered, and stepped behind Orlaith. Orlaith glared at Callum.

'Why don't *you* kill it?' she said.

'Because shut up,' he snapped. He clutched at his growling stomach. 'Please, somebody just kill it. *I can't take it any more!*'

We knew how he felt. The last twenty-four hours had been difficult on everyone. It turned out the forest hadn't been filled with berries and warthog like Callum had promised. There had been lots of mosquitoes, though.

'Hey!' Callum cried. '*Look!*'

He pointed at the sheep in disbelief. It was tearing up a clutch of grass that sprouted between the rocks and chewing it. Callum's eyes brightened.

'That's it!' he cried joyously. '*Grass!*'

He threw himself down onto his hands and knees and started furiously tearing grass straight out of the ground with his mouth. We watched him in stunned silence.

'I think he's eating a thistle,' said Ceri.

'Let him,' said Orlaith.

We dropped our bikes and slumped down onto the cold and clammy rocks. Callum wasn't the only one in our group that looked completely demented. None of us had known a thing about camping outside. In the cold and the dark, it had been impossible to see where we were going. We had spent every moment convinced that a bear was right behind us, waiting to pounce. Our hair had quickly filled with twigs, our clothes snagged on thorns and smeared with fox poo.

And then, of course, it had started raining.

'This isn't exactly what I expected from our adventure,' I muttered.

Orlaith stood up woozily.

'Well, I'm going to take the stormtrap up to higher ground,' she said. She gave it a vicious thump. 'Maybe then this piece of *junk* can start getting some signal again and we can work out where the tornado is.'

The stormtrap had been acting up ever since it started raining. Orlaith set off sluggishly up the quarry, heaving her bike with difficulty up the wet limestone. I sat with Ceri, swaying slightly with exhaustion. Up ahead Callum was trying to force Pete to murder the sheep, despite the fact Pete was crying and insisting that he was a Vegetable Aryan.

We sat in silence for a while. I glanced at Ceri. She was staring blankly at the ground. Her white hair was pasted to her forehead in thin strands, and her back was hunched against the rain. She was rubbing her legs.

'You alright?' I said.

170

She looked up sluggishly. 'Hmm? What?'

I glanced back down at her legs.

'You're being very quiet,' I said. 'Not feeling too . . . tired?'

She shook her head. 'Oh no, I'm fine! Totally, completely fine. I just . . .' She let out a deep sigh. 'I just miss Flossie, that's all.'

I blinked. 'Really?'

Ceri nodded. 'Of course. She's my little sister.' She scratched despondently at a block of wet stone in front of her. 'It's my job to look after her, you know? To make sure she's safe. And if I'm not doing it . . . I mean, who is?'

We fell silent again. Up ahead Callum and Pete were attempting to outsmart the sheep by chasing it round a tree. It wasn't going very well. I glanced back at Ceri. She was rubbing her legs again.

'You're sure that's all it is?' I said.

Ceri fixed me with a look. 'What do you mean?'

I pointed at her legs.

'You keep rubbing them.' I paused. 'We can . . . stop for a bit, you know, Ceri.'

She clenched her jaw irritably. 'We *can't* actually, Owen. We have to keep going.'

She got to her feet, her face flashing with discomfort,

and made her way awkwardly up the quarry. I ran after her.

'Ceri,' I said, 'you can't just be brave for the sake of it. If they hurt, then you should say somethi—'

I made to put my hand on her shoulder. In a flash she swung round and smacked it away. I startled. The two of us fell silent.

'You . . . you didn't have to do that,' I said, rubbing my hand. 'I was trying to help you.'

'Well, you weren't helping!' said Ceri. 'You were making me feel like a problem.'

We looked at each other in the rain. The water dripped down into the back of my collar. I twitched, despite myself.

'Sorry,' I said quietly. 'I didn't mean to. I know what it's like when . . . well, I know what it's like when people think you can't do anything.'

Ceri's face softened, just slightly. She sighed, and wiped the strands of wet hair from her forehead.

'Alright, alright,' she grumbled. 'I didn't mean to snap at you. It's just the braces. I'm not supposed to get them wet, and now they're giving me blisters.'

I smiled. 'Really? That's it? Blisters?'

Ceri nodded. 'Massive ones. Seriously, check them out! They're like little faces!'

She loosened one of the straps and showed me the

welt beside her knee. I grimaced.

'That's really gross, Ceri,' I said.

'Yeah!' she said brightly. 'I know!'

We fell silent again. The rain drummed down around us. In the distance Pete had the sheep in a headlock.

'Do you reckon we'll get to the tornado in time?' said Ceri. 'Before it passes by Skirting, I mean?'

I thought about it.

'I'm not sure.'

'Me neither,' said Ceri. She nudged me with her elbow. 'Still, I'm glad we're doing it anyway.'

I smiled. 'Yeah. Me too.'

'You *WHAT*?'

We froze. The scream had come from the top of the quarry. It was Callum. We made our way quickly up the slope.

Orlaith and Callum were facing each other, the wind and rain pelting furiously against them. Up here we could feel the strength of the tornado again, heaving against us and sending our sopping wet capes flapping in the rain behind us. In the distance the sheep had managed to climb a tree and was sitting calmly on a branch while Pete attempted to poke it off with a stick.

'You must be out of your mind!' Callum shouted at Orlaith.

Orlaith waved the stormtrap in front of him. 'I *told* you, the trap's not had any signal all day! We can't just stop and wait for it to come back! We have to keep moving!'

'What's going on?' I said, stepping between them. 'What's the problem?'

Callum's eyes bugged out of his head. He pointed to the horizon.

'*That!*' he cried.

We looked across the valleys ahead of us. There wasn't much you could see through the clouds that now whipped through the landscape, blanketing everything in a dull white. We could just make out the great mountain range that separated the valleys from the North. They were much closer now. They crouched in the clouds like ancient giants, their surface streaked with scars and scored with ragged drops on either side.

'*That's* where she's taking us!' Callum cried accusingly.

Orlaith sighed. 'Look, I already explained – we're not going anywhere near the Caves! But we're going to have to go *towards* them, aren't we? I mean, we're heading north . . . !'

Ceri blinked. 'I don't get it. What's wrong with the Caves?'

'What's *wrong* with the Great North Caves?' Callum gasped incredulously. 'Don't you even *listen* in class?'

We stared at him. It wasn't a sentence we had ever imagined him saying.

'*The Great North Caves?*' he said, waving his arms. 'Otherwise known as *The Bear Caves?*'

I startled, and glanced at the great white rock face ahead of us in shock.

'That's . . . where all the bears live?' I whispered, my voice tight with fear.

Orlaith put her hands on her hips. 'Well, if we *don't* head towards them now the stormtrap's broken, we'll get lost! And if we get lost, we'll run out of time before the tornado passes us. Besides – we've still got two cans of repellent! And we haven't seen a single bear yet, have we?'

We glanced at each other. It was true – there hadn't been any sign of them. But Callum was having none of it.

'Two cans of repellent aren't going to make any difference out here!' he ranted. 'We might as well cover ourselves in sauce and offer ourselves up to the bears on a platter!'

'That sounds quite fun, actually,' said Ceri.

'*It's not fun!*' Callum fumed.

He stepped towards us, his eyes clamped wide open. I couldn't help but step away from him. He looked unhinged.

'Don't you know what they *do* when they find a child?'

No one answered him. He fixed his gaze on us for a

while, then turned around and faced the valleys. The wind roared up the hillside and beat against him, but he didn't seem to notice.

'Callum,' I said nervously. 'Callum, come away from the edge.'

He didn't reply. A distant look had come over him.

'They never kill them first,' he said. His voice was suddenly quiet. 'Oh no. They drag them back to the caves. They take them inside, for the others to see.'

There was another bellow of wind, and a wall of bleach-white clouds crept over the stones at Callum's feet.

'There's nothing but tunnels inside,' came Callum's voice from the clouds ahead. 'Pitch-black, dead ends. Only the bears know their way around them.'

The clouds had surrounded us entirely. I glanced at the others through the fog. We had never heard him talk like this before. He stood, motionless, as the wind roared and rattled around him. It was getting stronger now, louder, colder.

'Even if you did manage to escape from the bears,' said Callum, 'you'd never find your way outside again. You'd only end up deeper in the mountain. Nothing but rocks a mile above you and a mile below you. No one would ever find you. They wouldn't even be able to hear you scream.'

176

He paused.

'They say the ones in the centre, the furthest inside, are just filled with bones and hair . . .'

Orlaith suddenly ran forwards and grabbed him.

'Callum, *stop it*!' she said. 'You're frightening everyone!'

Callum pulled free of her grip. '*I'm* frightening everyone? You're the one who's leading us right to them!'

The clouds wrapped thicker and thicker around us, smothering our skin in freezing dampness and blinding us from one another. Our group was falling apart and there was nothing we could do. In the tree behind us we could just make out Pete trying to convince the sheep to jump.

'Oh, and well then how about you?' snapped Orlaith. 'Mr "I'm Not Afraid Of Anything"? Why don't you take charge, seeing as you're so much braver than everyone else?'

I fumbled forwards, trying to find them. 'Come on, guys – maybe if we all sit down like grown-ups, and have a chat about it . . .'

There was a sudden *thump* behind us, followed by a wail. I turned round.

'. . . Pete?' I said. 'Pete, was that you?'

There was no reply. The others hadn't even noticed.

'I'll tell you what the problem is,' came Callum's voice in the fog. 'The problem is that you pretend like you know exactly what to do, with all your plans and stupid inventions, but look at us! We haven't eaten or slept in two days!'

I turned away from them, and stepped towards the tree.

'Pete? Are you OK?'

'Well you know what, Callum?' came Orlaith's voice. 'That's just what happens! We're not in an adventure story!'

The sheep flew out of the fog towards me, stumbling down the stones into the distance, bleating in fear. I startled wildly, and looked towards the tree. It stood in the mist before me like a skeletal hand, clawing up from the stones, trembling in the wind. My heart began to pound.

'P-Pete?' I said. 'Pete, are you there?'

'Sometimes you *have* to get lost!' Orlaith cried. 'And cold! And hungry!'

Pete was on the ground beneath the tree, lying on his back. I knelt down beside him.

'Pete!' I said. 'Pete, what happened?'

'Something fell on me,' he groaned. 'Out the sky.'

I glanced down. There was something lying on the ground next to him.

'Sometimes, nothing works out how you want it to!'

I reached down and picked it up.

It was a teddy bear.

'You can't just get whatever you want!'

At that moment something fell to the ground beside me with a soft thump. I stared at it.

It was a tasselled silk cushion.

'Because *that's real life!*'

All at once, the clouds passed, and the sun came out, and the stones around me emerged into view. I gasped. Pillows and cushions and blankets and duvets were falling from the sky in every direction, tumbling down the rocky slopes and heaping in piles at our feet, covering the quarry.

'Nobody's going to turn up and magically fix everything for you!'

The downfall stopped, as quickly as it started. I gazed out in stunned silence at the quarry before me. It was filled with brightly coloured comfortable bedding, dotted with teddy bears and rugs and rocking horses.

'And you know what, Callum? Food doesn't just appear out of the sky!'

And that was when it started raining biscuits.

17

A Change in Plan

It had stopped raining biscuits.

We sat on the edge of the quarry, looking out across the countryside. It was quite a sight now the clouds had finally cleared. The valleys to the East were a sea of yellow rubber ducks. Blankets and feathery pillows were strewn for miles and miles in either direction, turning the furthest treetops into great circuses of colour. The hillside we sat on was decked with thousands upon thousands of wedding dresses.

The tornado lay on the horizon. It had doubled in size since the first day we saw it. The clouds had now stained a darker grey, funnelling into jet blackness as they wormed their way to the ground. In its wake lay the remains of half a dozen destroyed factories, their contents scattered for miles in every direction.

'It doesn't *look* like it's heading this way,' I said, chewing on a flapjack.

Orlaith took a bite of her Victoria sponge.

'That's because it's, er . . . not,' she mumbled, spraying crumbs.

'Oh yeah,' said Ceri, licking the icing off a cupcake. 'And it wasn't supposed to go near the factories either, was it?'

'No,' said Orlaith sheepishly. 'It wasn't. But it looks like it, er . . . pulled away from the stormtraps. I guess the tornado was just too strong for them to control it.'

'Huh,' said Callum, jamming an entire doughnut into his mouth. 'Well, it's been a pretty good result for us, anyway.'

It was true. The storm going unexpectedly off-course and devastating several dozen factories had been an absolute triumph for the Tornado Chasers. We had feasted on cakes and buns and biscuits until we'd been sick, before napping the nap of kings in a giant nest of throw-cushions that had collected in the quarry. I had woken up in glorious midday sunshine to find Pete sharing a wedding cake with the sheep, their old rivalry a distant memory.

'Well,' muttered Orlaith nervously. 'Not *that* good.'

We looked at her. Callum swallowed his doughnut whole, with some difficulty.

'Why?' he managed to choke out.

Orlaith held up the stormtrap. It had finally got its signal back.

'The tornado's left the path it was on,' she said. 'It broke away from the stormtraps and went on a rampage through the countryside. Luckily it got picked up by another set of stormtraps – but *look*.'

She rubbed a sleeve across the display and cleared the pen lines, before re-sketching the new path across the grid.

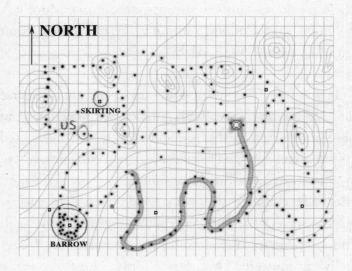

'It's going to keep going North, now,' she said, putting the marker pen back in her pocket. 'It's not going to head towards us any more.'

She trailed off. We sat in silence, watching the distant tower of clouds as they wound away from us. We had underestimated the tornado. All of a sudden it seemed very far away again.

'Isn't there somewhere else we can cut it off?' said Ceri.

Orlaith sighed. 'Well, now it's going to run over to the north side of Skirting, before being funnelled up away from the valleys . . .'

'The other side of Skirting?' Callum cried. 'But . . . we'll never get around the village in time!'

Orlaith shook her head.

'We will,' she said defiantly, 'if we walk *through* it. That way, there's still a good chance we can cut off the tornado when it passes by on the North side tomorrow morning.'

Everyone signed with relief – except me.

'*No!*' I cried, startling massively.

Everyone turned to look at me. I shook the twitch out of my neck, slightly surprised at myself.

'I . . . I can't go through Skirting,' I mumbled. 'I used to live there.'

Callum frowned. 'So? Everyone's going to be shut up indoors, Owen. There's a tornado right outside their valley!'

'But . . . I could still be recognised!' I protested. 'I mean, if someone looks out of a window and sees me, even for a second . . . They must have put out a notice across the valleys for us by now, right? And people in Skirting will know what I look like!'

The others shared a glance.

'He's right.' Orlaith sighed. 'We have to make sure no one recognises him.'

Callum frowned. 'What about the rest of us? We'll need to be in disguise, too!'

'Yeah,' said Ceri. 'I mean, Orlaith – you look *exactly* like your dad.'

Orlaith flushed. 'No I don't! We look completely different!'

'Oh, right,' said Ceri, nodding. 'Except for your hair. And your eyes.'

'And your ears,' I added helpfully.

'Plus you're both black,' said Callum.

Orlaith glowered. 'Well – whatever! We're not going to be in an identity parade! We just need to make sure no one recognises Owen! Sheesh!'

Everyone turned to look at me, scratching their chins like I was a tricky crossword puzzle.

'Well, he doesn't have that helmet any more, does he?' said Ceri, as if I wasn't there. 'Maybe without it people won't remember him.'

Orlaith shook her head. 'Not enough. We need to make him look so different, no one would even consider it was him.'

Ceri shrugged. 'Well – maybe he could put on some different clothes, too?'

Callum snorted. 'Oh yeah, great idea, Ceri! Let's just use all those extra clothes we have magically lying around out here, on a hillside in the middle of nowhere . . . !'

He cast his arm around him, and stopped. He gazed at the hundreds of wedding dresses that covered almost every inch of grass on the hillside beside us. He looked at the others. They smiled.

My face fell.

'Er,' I said. 'Look, I don't mean to be difficult, but I really would rather not wear a wedding dress – if you don't mind.'

The others didn't say anything. They were still smiling.

'Guys? Did you hear me?'

They started walking towards me. I swallowed.

'. . . Guys?'

18

Skirting on the Edge of Danger

'You look lovely, Owen.'

'Thanks.'

'Now pull down the veil.'

I reluctantly adjusted my headpiece. Ceri stepped back with a satisfied grin. Everyone nodded appreciatively, with the exception of Callum who was bent double with laughter against a nearby tree.

'I still don't see how this is going to make me stand out less,' I mumbled sheepishly.

Ceri sighed. 'Owen, for the hundredth time! So long as people don't see it's *you*, it's an improvement. Consider it just like wearing the cape. Except white and frilly. And – if I say so myself – very flattering on the waist.'

I held out a bunch of plastic posies.

'Can I at least lose the bouquet?' I begged.

'First rule of undercover reporting,' said Ceri, shoving them back into my hand. 'The details matter.'

We were on the valley floor, crouched behind the hedges that surrounded Skirting. The road that led through town was barely a stone's throw away. Orlaith pulled everyone together into a huddle, including Callum, who was still wiping tears from his face and struggling to breathe.

'Now listen,' she said. 'I've been doing some thinking, and I'm afraid we're going to have to leave the bikes behind.'

Everyone made to protest, but Orlaith waved us quiet.

'We don't have a choice,' she said. 'Their chains got wet and they're squeaking. We can't risk anyone hearing us when we go through Skirting. We'll have to go on foot from now on. We can pick everything up again on our way back.'

Callum quickly glanced up. 'Hang on – what about Ceri? How's she going to walk?'

Ceri shrugged. 'I can walk it.'

Orlaith bit her lip. 'We'll . . . we'll need to be fast, Ceri. We've only got until tomorrow morning to get onto the other side of that hill.'

She pointed at the valley beyond Skirting, where clouds were already beginning to darken in anticipation of the approaching tornado.

'Maybe . . . maybe it'd be better if someone carried you,' she suggested carefully.

Pete put a hand on Ceri's shoulder.

'I don't mind doing it,' he said gently.

Ceri smiled. 'Thank you, Pete, that's very sweet of you. But if you *ever* try to pick me up, I'm going to punch you in the face.'

Pete squeaked and backed away. Ceri nodded at us. The matter was apparently closed. Orlaith shrugged.

'Fair enough.' She turned to me. 'Look round the corner, Owen. Is it clear?'

I peered around the hedge. There was no sign of anyone patrolling the streets. The town looked still, and silent. I smiled.

'Hey! I know this road!' I whispered excitedly. 'Look – there's the baker's! And the pub! And *that* corner right there goes to the high street!'

I turned to the others, my heart racing. It was nice to finally be the one who knew what to do.

'If we go down there, we can get to the church in the main square,' I said. 'That'll lead us out the other side of town.'

Orlaith nodded. 'Perfect. We'll go one at a time – Owen, you can lead. You'll know your way around Skirting better than all of us.'

I checked round the hedge again – the coast was clear. I adjusted my veil with authority.

'Ready?' I whispered to the others.

They nodded. I lifted up my skirts, crept out from the hedge, and zipped along the edge of the road. I came to a stop by the bakery, crouching down beside a wall. Orlaith quickly arrived behind me, followed by the others. I glanced out across the road, my chest hammering. Still no sign of anyone.

'Right,' I said breathlessly. 'The high street's round the corner. Ready . . . ?'

'Hang on,' said Ceri. 'What's going on with their windows?'

She pointed to the houses opposite us. They looked – well, completely normal.

'They haven't stormboarded their windows,' Ceri explained. 'Look. Or their doors, either.'

She was right. Not one of the windows along the street had any boards over them. Some curtains hadn't even been closed. Empty milk bottles still stood on the doorsteps. In fact, the street looked *exactly* the same as when I lived there.

'Well . . . Skirting never seemed that bothered about tornadoes, to be honest,' I said. 'It's not like Barrow.'

'Exactly,' said Orlaith sternly. 'We don't know *what* precautions they've taken for it. They might all be in a bunker in the centre of town. Right, Owen?'

Everyone looked at me expectantly. I fumbled.

'Er . . . yeah, I guess they might be,' I said. 'Let's just keep going.'

Everyone nodded. I took a deep breath, and shot out from beside the bins, the uneasiness in my chest growing and growing. It was strange to be back in Skirting – even stranger to be doing it like this, in secret. And now I was about to see the high street again. I couldn't put my finger on it. It was like being in a dream, or a past life. Maybe that was why something felt so *wrong* . . .

I turned the corner, and stopped.

The high street ahead of me was exactly as I remembered it. The post office, the butcher's, the newsagent, the restaurants, were all in exactly the same places.

They were also open.

The street ahead was full of people.

Orlaith crashed into the back of me, sending me sprawling to the ground. She gawped ahead of her in disbelief.

'*What?*' she cried.

Callum came to a stumbling stop beside her, his mouth hanging open. Then came Pete, and finally Ceri. We gazed at the busy street ahead of us in shock. The people of Skirting were going about their daily business, shopping and running errands and stopping for chats. It was like they had no idea that a tornado was right on their doorstep.

'Owen,' Callum hissed, 'what the *hell* is going on?'

'I ... I don't know!' I said, my eyes searching the street for some sort of explanation. 'Why are they ... why are they all outside?'

My stomach dropped. The reality of what was happening suddenly dawned on me. Maybe people in Skirting didn't care at all about the tornado. Maybe I was standing in the middle of a busy street, in a town where people knew my face, while I was on the run. And wearing a wedding dress.

'Excuse me,' said a voice from right behind us. 'Are you children lost?'

I startled – or rather, I *almost* startled. I just managed to hold it back at the last minute. Behind me stood an old woman, wearing a peacock-blue skirt suit and a fancy feathered hat. She was carrying big bags of shopping in each hand.

'*Are you lost?*' the old lady repeated, a little louder.

'You seem a little confused. Are you from round here?'

I squeaked, and whipped the veil down over my face. People were stopping in the street and turning to look at us, nudging each other, pointing. I started to panic. Sweat beaded down my forehead. If I startled now, and somebody recognised me . . .

The bottom of one of the woman's shopping bags suddenly fell through, scattering her food across the road. I clenched my jaw shut, forcing the twitch down into my fists and toes and guts. It took all the strength I had. The old woman tutted, looking down at her spilled shopping on the cobblestones.

'Oh my *goodness* me!' she squeaked. 'These thin plastic bags are just hopeless! What a mess. I couldn't possibly carry all this myself . . .'

Pete's face suddenly lit up. He ran forwards and scooped up the old lady's shopping into his arms. The old lady clucked in approval.

'Ooh!' she said. 'What a polite young man! And so strong!' She patted him warmly on the shoulder. 'Thank you ever so much, my dear.'

Pete glowed.

'You're welcome, miss,' he said, looking at her with an expression I hadn't seen on him before.

The people around us in the street started slowly

turning away, their attentions taken up by other things. Just five weird kids helping out an old lady – nothing to see here. I breathed a sigh of relief. The woman turned to us gratefully.

'Would you children be so kind as to carry them to the end of the street for me?' she asked. 'I'm supposed to be meeting my daughter for lunch, and I'm already running late. She's not been at all well lately, you see . . .'

'Of course we'll go with you!' said Orlaith, leaping forwards. 'We were heading to the main square anyway – weren't we, guys?'

The old lady turned to me and smiled.

'Ah! Well, of *course* you are,' she said, pointing at me. 'I suppose this dress is to celebrate the wedding, is it? What fun!'

I nodded wildly, even though I had no idea what she was talking about. The old lady suddenly frowned, and looked at me in confusion.

'Hang on a moment,' she said, peering at my face. 'Don't I know you . . . ?'

Pete thrust the shopping bags into my hands and grabbed one of the old lady's arms, wheeling her away down the street.

'You shouldn't be carrying around shopping at your age,' he muttered, his voice suddenly warm and protective. 'It won't be doing your back any favours, will it? Let's get you going – your daughter must be wondering where you are!'

We looked at each other in disbelief. Pete was an expert nan-talker. And what's more, it was working perfectly. With the old lady beside us, nobody in the street seemed to bat an eyelid. It was as if we just blended in with the rest of Skirting. No one even seemed to be bothered that I was wearing a wedding dress. I gazed at them in utter bewilderment through my veil. *Why were they still outside?*

'So nice of you children to help me,' the old lady was saying warmly. 'You know, I paid ten pence each for those bags! Ten pence!'

'What? You never,' tutted Pete, genuinely shocked.

'Dreadful,' said Ceri, scampering forwards. 'I mean, really. You should write a letter. So . . . the high street certainly seems busy today, doesn't it?'

She pointed ahead. There was a crowd at the main square, cheering and jostling excitedly.

'Well, it would be!' said the old lady. 'There's a big wedding at the church today! I thought I'd bring my daughter outside to see it – although she does so *hate* being outside at the moment . . .'

'Quite,' said Orlaith, struggling to hide her boredom.

194

'But . . . they're having a *wedding*? *Today*? And no one's worried about the tornado?'

The old lady turned to look at Orlaith quizzically.

'The *tornado*?' she repeated. 'Well, no dear. It's on the other side of the hill. It'll do us no harm here.'

We glanced at each other.

'But . . . it just broke away from the stormtraps and wrecked a load of factories!' said Callum.

'Oh yes, *that*,' said the old lady with a sigh. 'They were talking about it on the radio this morning. An old faulty stormtrap, they said! Nothing there to push the tornado onto the next one, so it broke away from the chain. Luckily, our one is working perfectly.'

She pointed to the church spire, where a single stormtrap blinked in the sun. We looked at each other in confusion.

'But . . . shouldn't you all be inside anyway?' I said. 'You know – just to be on the safe side? I mean . . . the bears are still going to be roaming the valleys, aren't they?'

The old lady looked at me, her brow furrowing.

'Where did you children say you were from again?' she muttered.

I froze. Orlaith quickly stepped forwards.

'Oh, nothing!' She laughed, wheeling the old lady

195

away from me. 'Just . . . wondering aloud. You know what they say – better safe than sorry!'

The old lady laughed.

'You sound just like my daughter!' she said. 'Always worrying about safety. I'll tell you, we had quite a fight getting *her* to leave her house and come to Skirting during the storm . . . She thinks she should be back in her house, digging herself into the basement. But it's like I told her yesterday – Victoria, a few weeks out of that nasty village and away from all those vicious rumours about your mental health will sort you out in no time . . . oh look, here she is now!'

We turned around. Stood in the middle of the street behind us, mouth hanging open, was Miss Pewlish.

I startled. BIG time. My arms swung the bags of shopping around like Catherine wheels and they split in mid-air, scattering eggs and bottles in a wide arc and sending them shattering onto the tarmac. A whole watermelon hit the ground with a great meaty *THUNK* and bounced along the pavement. The crowds swung round to face us, staring at Miss Pewlish as she opened and closed her mouth like someone wolfing down a hearty stew of confusion, shock and rage. The old lady suddenly stepped forwards.

'Victoria!' she said. 'I just met the *nicest* young children, you simply *must* say hello . . .'

Miss Pewlish shoved her aside and faced us.

'*That's them!*' she bellowed. '*The Tornado Chasers!* SOMEONE ARREST THESE CHILDREN!'

The people in the crowd around us looked puzzled. Some even started laughing. The old lady shot them a furious glare, and patted Miss Pewlish on the shoulder with motherly concern.

'Yes, dear,' she said. 'Of course they are. The Tornado Chasers. Perhaps we should get you home now. Looks like being outside has, er . . . overexcited you.' She turned to us and gave us a wink. 'You lot run off now. I don't think she knows what she's saying . . .'

'*ATTENTION PLEASE.*'

The voice came through a loudspeaker behind us, echoing down the streets. The crowds muttered with confusion, and parted. At the end of the road stood a convoy of black vans. On the side of each one, in great white letters, was written COUNTY DETENTION CENTRE. My stomach fell.

'Oh dear,' I whispered.

A group of burly men in black uniforms stepped out of the vans. They wore black gloves and carried truncheons and handcuffs. The one at the front lifted the loudspeaker up to his mouth.

'YOUR ATTENTION PLEASE,' he repeated.

'WE ARE CURRENTLY SEARCHING FOR FIVE CHILDREN WHO HAVE RUN AWAY FROM THEIR HOMES IN BARROW. I REPEAT, IF ANYONE HAS SEEN *FIVE CHILDREN* . . .'

The crowd gasped, and turned to us. Fingers were pointed. The old lady looked at us in confusion. I gulped.

'Er . . . guys?' I muttered. 'What do we . . .'

'*PEG IT!*' Callum screamed.

He sprang up the street like a rocket, barging through the crowds and sending people either side of him tumbling to the ground. Before I knew what was happening Orlaith had followed, and Pete had thrown down his shopping and raced after her. Ceri leapt up and down in panic.

'*Pete!*' she cried. '*For Christ's sake, get back here and carry me!*'

Pete ran back and threw Ceri over his shoulder before charging away through the crowd. Miss Pewlish finally pulled herself together enough to leap into action.

'*Right here, officers!*' she cried, waving her arms. '*I'll catch them!*'

Miss Pewlish made to grab me, but I dodged out the way at the last second and shot up the street away from her. She roared and flew after me, but immediately plunged her foot into the watermelon and flipped over

198

backwards with a terrible shriek, somersaulting through the air several times and bellowing like a faulty firework before finally landing head first in a nearby bin.

'*Quick! Grab him!*'

The County officers sprinted up the street after me. I charged through the confused and shouting crowds around the square, barrelling through their legs, my head darting this way and that.

'*Orlaith! Ceri! Pete! Callum! Where are . . .*'

I suddenly fell out the other side and sprawled across the cobblestones. I was on the main square. The crowds had parted for the wedding ceremony, and up ahead I could make out Callum and Orlaith and Pete scrambling round the corner of the church. Ceri was still slung over Pete's shoulder. She pointed behind me.

'*Owen, look out!*'

I turned round to see two County officers heaving through the crowd and waving their truncheons at me.

'That's him!' said the one at the front. 'The one in the wedding dress! Someone stop him!'

Without another word a dozen men flew from the crowd and raced after me. Someone tried to grab my veil, but I managed to wrench myself free and flew around the corner after the others. They had come to a stop up ahead. The bride and groom had emerged from the church doors to rapturous applause, and the crowds were massed together, cheering and crying and waving flags and blocking the path.

'*Straight ahead!*' I bellowed to the others. '*There's a road on the other side that leads to the hills! Quick, they're right behind me!*'

Pete nodded, and with a grunt threw himself into the crowd, barging people left and right. We followed at high speed. In front of us, the bride and groom were posing for their official photograph beside an enormous pyramid of champagne glasses and a lavish hog roast buffet. We flew past them just as the photograph was taken, to cries of horror and disapproval from the wedding party. At that exact moment, the men in pursuit of us appeared round the corner of the church. The County officer at the front pointed at me as I disappeared through the crowd.

'*That's him!*' he cried. '*Right there! He's getting away!*'

The chasing men looked confused. 'Which one?'

The County officer jumped up and down. '*The one in the wedding dress!*'

Without further ado the men flew forward, rugby tackling the bride to the ground and sending the groom flying into the tower of glasses. The hog roast was overturned and immediately savaged by a pack of stray cats that had been waiting at the sidelines for such an opportunity. The wedding party – having sat all morning through an excruciating church service, only to see their well-earned champagne and roast pork cruelly torn away from them at the last minute – clamoured for blood, heaving forwards in a wave of violent, hungry retribution. Punches were swung and handbags whirled round heads and bouquets used as clubs. Someone threw a bridesmaid. The lead County officer tried to run after us, but his attempts at escape were blocked by a pair of enraged maiden aunts who were standing in front of him and jabbing him with hatpins.

'*Someone – ouch! – stop those – ouch! – children!*' he cried.

It was no good. We had already disappeared around the corner and were running down an empty side street, out of Skirting and into the hills as fast as we could.

19

The House

We tumbled down the valley slope in the driving rain, our clothes soaked and stained with mud. We hadn't stopped running since we left Skirting – and that was hours ago. Orlaith had dragged us on all day, her sights fixed on the black mass of clouds that slowly grew closer and closer in the distance. Above us the thunder cracked, and the trees were blasted with a gust of freezing wind.

'Please!' Callum begged, waving his arms weakly. 'Let's rest! Just for a moment!'

He threw himself against a tree beside me, groaning with pain. I came to a slow and graceless stop beside him, bending over double with exhaustion. Pete put Ceri down on the ground and collapsed like a cow into the mud. Orlaith finally came to a stop ahead of us, leaning forwards on her knees.

'Alright,' she sighed. 'We can stop now. It doesn't look like we're being followed. I was worried we wouldn't even make it this far, but look – the tornado's still miles away!'

She pointed through the trees, to the distant bank of clouds.

'It won't pass through the valley below until tomorrow morning!' she said triumphantly. 'We can rest here for tonight.'

She put her hands on her hips and faced us. We glanced at each other.

'Er . . . Orlaith?' said Ceri. 'Rest . . . *where* exactly?'

The forest around us was descending into blackness. We were outside with night coming fast, right beside the Great North Caves. A fresh sheet of freezing rain suddenly blasted through the trees, spraying us with leaves and dirt. From further down the valley came the creaking of branches. We jumped. There could be bears anywhere around us – hundreds of them. Orlaith swallowed nervously.

'Well . . . I suppose we'll just have to sleep rough for one more night.' She turned to me. 'After all, we've still got all that bear repellent with us – haven't we, Owen?'

Everyone's eyes fixed on me. I reached for my pockets, and my stomach dropped.

'Oh no,' I said.

The cans were in my shorts, back in the sidecar of Pete's bike – the other side of Skirting. I looked at the others in horror.

'We've got nothing,' I said, my voice taut and panicked. 'We . . . we have to find shelter, quick!'

Callum's eyes boggled. '*Shelter?* Are you kidding? Look at this place! Where the *hell* are we going to find a proper shelter now, right here in the middle of nowhere . . . ?'

Ceri pointed to the distance. 'Well, we could always try that house over there.'

We turned around.

'Oh,' I said.

In the middle of the forest below us was a house. It was made of bricks, with a roof and a chimney and four perfect square windows. It was unusual to see it here on the other side of the valleys, in the centre of a clearing of trees, with no path leading up to it.

It was also unusual because it was lying on its side.

We stared at the house for some time. It was Callum who eventually broke the silence.

'What the hell is that,' he said.

We walked cautiously up to the house, and peeked

through the windows. There were no lights on inside. The windowpanes were laced with cobwebs.

'Look at it,' said Orlaith. 'It must have been here for years. Maybe since the last tornado, even.'

I shivered. 'Well, it looks warm. There could be dry clothes in there, too.'

'And food,' added Ceri.

We stood in silence. Around us, the rain pounded down.

'Do you reckon . . . there's anyone still inside?' said Callum.

Orlaith gulped. 'Someone should go and check.'

'Yeah,' said Callum. 'Someone.'

There was another prolonged silence.

'Well, someone go inside already,' Callum snapped.

I gulped. 'Maybe . . . maybe we should draw straws for it.'

'A democratic vote would be better,' said Orlaith nervously.

'I vote Owen,' said Callum.

'Hey, guys! In here!'

We turned around, and nearly leapt out of our skins. Ceri was already stood on the other side of the window, waving at us cheerfully.

'Ceri!' I gasped. 'How did you . . . ?'

'Chimney!' she said, pointing over at the side of the house. We glanced over. Sure enough, the house's chimney stuck out the roof at ground level beside us. 'Just crawl through! It's really nice in here. And get this – the *ceiling* is a *wall* and the *wall* has a *carpet* on it. How cool is that?'

We crawled through the chimney, one by one, and emerged from the fireplace into the living room. It was uncanny. The doorways, the lights, the windows, the wallpaper – all old and faded, but perfectly preserved. Even the carpet on the floor – which, true to Ceri's word, was now a wall – was still soft. The only difference was that everything was on its side. The contents of the living room lay spread around us in great broken piles, covered by a thick layer of dust.

'Pretty cool, isn't it?' said Ceri. 'Bit messy, but I guess we could make some room to lie down next to this broken glass here . . .'

Pete suddenly marched to the centre of the room and pushed her aside, kneeling down on the floor where she had been standing. We watched in confusion as he rooted through the piles of broken picture frames at her feet. It was like he was looking for something. He suddenly heaved aside a pile of rubbish, and magically revealed a single wooden door on the floor. He swung it open and lowered himself through into the room below. Within seconds we could hear the clattering of saucepans and the slamming of cupboard beneath us.

'Er . . . Pete?' I said, leaning over the hole in the floor. 'You alright down there . . . ?'

Pete suddenly re-emerged at the doorway and clambered back out. In his hands were a mop and bucket, a dustpan and broom, and a duster. He pulled on a pair of yellow rubber gloves and turned to us.

'Get some dry clothes,' he said. 'I'll sort this out.'

He had already flapped open a recycling bag and was filling it with tatty old magazines from the floor. We glanced at each other.

'Pete, are you sure . . . ?' Orlaith began.

'Busy,' he said, hurrying us outside. 'Shoo.'

Getting upstairs was easier said than done, given that the staircase was now on its side. We had to lower ourselves into the bedrooms to search for old clothes. There were plenty scattered inside, but none for children. Whoever lived here once was old, and long gone. We found some dusty suits and shirts that were two sizes too big for us, and clambered back down to the living room.

We gazed in disbelief at what Pete had done in the short time we were away. The chaos of broken furniture had been completely cleared. In its place was a circle of sofas and armchairs, arranged like a camp at the centre of the room. A bonfire of old books was gently kindling in the sideways fireplace, the warm light flickering through coloured bed sheets and velvet curtains draped from the ceiling. On top of the fireplace sat a makeshift stove, made from the upturned grate. A dozen carefully opened tins of soup stood bubbling gently on top, filling the room with the smell of leek and potato.

Pete suddenly emerged from the hole in the floor, wearing an apron and carrying an old sack of potatoes. He looked us up and down in our baggy, dusty clothes, and frowned.

'I hope you washed your hands,' he muttered.

We sat on the sofas and warmed ourselves through with mug after mug of piping-hot soup while the wind howled outside, rattling the windowpanes. We picked the tubers off the old potatoes and wrapped the potatoes in foil, baking them in the embers of the fireplace until they piped and squealed and we couldn't bear to wait any longer. We ate them in silence, with no butter. Afterwards we lay back on the sofas, passing around a tin of fruit cocktail.

'I think that might have been the best meal I've had in my life,' I said.

Everyone muttered in agreement. We were full, and we were dry, and we had done it all ourselves. We were happy. Orlaith stretched out lazily, like a cat.

'We should get some sleep,' she said. 'We all need to be up first thing tomorrow.'

We arranged the bedding around the sofas, and clambered into place. The fire was slowly dying, and the room was cast in oranges and dull browns around us. Pete found a set of pyjamas in an upstairs bedroom and joined us on a sofa, the springs squealing and dipping as he lay down. We lay on our backs, watching the fire lines dance on the ceiling and walls around us.

'So this is it,' said Ceri excitedly. 'Our last night before the tornado.'

The information settled on us. I don't think any of us had ever expected to find ourselves here together, so far from home, so close to the end.

'What do you think it'll be like?' said Ceri.

We turned to look at her.

'The tornado,' she said. 'When we're next to it. What do you think it'll feel like?'

We thought about it.

'Windy,' said Pete.

'*Really* windy,' said Callum. 'Like in a film when there's a big explosion and everyone gets thrown backwards.'

'Actually, tornadoes draw you *in*,' I said. 'Like a whirlpool. And the bit in the middle is completely still.' I held my hands out flat. 'No wind at all. They call it the heart of the storm. It's when people think it's all over, but it's not – it's a trick. There's more to come.'

Callum rolled over, propping himself up with a cushion. 'Since when did you find out so much about tornadoes?'

I shrugged. 'My grandparents left lots of stuff behind. Books, flight notes . . . that kind of thing. They're all kept in cupboards and boxes in the attic, hidden out the way. My parents would be furious if they knew I'd looked through them.' I frowned. 'To be honest, I think they'd be angry if they found out I'd been up the attic ladder by myself.'

The others muttered in agreement.

'Tell me about it!' said Ceri. 'My dad keeps all the scissors in our house in a locked drawer. *All* of them. If I want to cut out paper I have to use my teeth.'

Callum turned round on the sofa. 'I don't get it. Why are all your parents such weirdoes about you lot being safe?'

Orlaith glanced at him. 'Yours aren't?'

Callum snorted. 'Ha! Are you joking? My parents are barely even at the house! It's just me and my babysi . . . I mean, my bodyguard.'

I shrugged. 'My parents have always been like that. I mean, it got worse when the valleys went under SW5, but still . . .' I thought about it. 'I guess it must have been hard for my dad as a child, watching his parents risk their lives all the time. Not knowing when they'd come home. Or even *if* they'd come home. Rather than make him adventurous too, it sort of . . . did the opposite.' I sighed. 'I guess that's why Barrow seemed so perfect for both of them. They wouldn't have to be worried about everything any more.'

Ceri nodded. 'Same for my parents. They didn't even used to live in Barrow, you know – they lived in High Bunting, then moved to Barrow when I was born. They were worried about my legs – they thought I wouldn't even be able to walk at one point. Now I can, and they don't even notice. They just think I won't be able to do *anything*. They don't even let me try.'

Pete sat up on the couch.

'We used to live in High Bunting, too,' he said with a smile. 'When my parents left, Nan moved us to Barrow. Where the tornadoes wouldn't hurt us.'

I sat up in confusion.

'Hang on,' I said. 'So – *all* of our parents moved to Barrow from other villages?'

Callum shook his head. 'No way! I've been around

since Barrow started. I mean, my dad's the one who built all the houses there, isn't he? That's why we're so loaded.'

Ceri spun round in shock. 'Wait – *that's* what your dad does? He . . . built Barrow?'

Callum nodded. 'Well, yeah. Him and some others. They put the houses there, and the ring of stormtraps around them, and said it was the safest village in the valleys and that no tornado could ever go near it. It was right after the last storm, wasn't it? So all these families who were frightened of tornadoes came pouring in. My dad made an absolute *packet* out of it.'

Orlaith looked at him coldly. 'And you're proud of that, are you?'

Callum shrugged. 'What – making money off scared people? Why wouldn't I be? It's their problem if they can't hack it.'

Orlaith looked away, chewing angrily at a fingernail. I shuffled on the cushion.

'What about you, Orlaith?' I said. 'Where did you used to live?'

She cleared her throat. 'Little Mews – my dad and my mum and me. Only right after I was born, my mum got really sick – no one saw it coming, and she just . . .'

She paused to quickly pick at her fingernails again, and let the words hang in the air.

212

'We moved to Barrow after she died. My dad blames himself for it, I think. Like if he'd been taking better care of all of us, if we'd been safer, then she'd still be here. That's why he's angry all the time. He doesn't mean to be. He's just . . . frightened.'

Callum glanced at her. 'Frightened? Of what?'

Orlaith looked at him. 'Of me dying, too.'

The sentence lay on our group like a lead weight. It was as if we had forgotten what the stakes were now – what could happen to us. We sat in silence for a moment.

'What about Skirting?' I said. 'Those people weren't frightened – were they?'

The others turned to look at me. I stared up at the ceiling that was really a wall.

'The tornado was right beside the village,' I said. 'And they were all outside. They were . . . *shopping*.'

I shook my head. It still didn't make any sense.

'I mean, that was the whole point of us doing this – right?' I said, turning to the others. 'To do something scary. To do something that no one else would dare to do. Only now, it turns out everyone in Skirting's been doing it all along.'

Silence fell on the group. No one had an answer for it.

'Maybe . . .' said Ceri. 'Maybe some people just don't care about that sort of thing, you know?'

Orlaith frowned. 'But how can you not care about *dying*?'

Ceri bit her lip. 'Maybe *anything's* better than living in fear.'

'As if,' muttered Callum. 'How can dying be better than anything?'

Pete shifted noisily on the sofa.

'At least when you die, you get to go to Heaven,' he said softly.

Orlaith glanced at him. 'Not everyone believes in Heaven, Pete.'

We lay in silence, watching the corners of the room dance and shift in the glow of the embers. Ceri rolled over and looked at us.

'What do you reckon it's like?' she said. 'Heaven. Or . . . the afterlife, whatever. Wherever it is you go when you die.'

No one answered her. She rolled onto her back again, looking at the ceiling and smiling.

'I reckon,' she said, 'you can do whatever you want. Like, you think of something and it just happens. And you can go anywhere– nothing can stop you. You just lift off the air and fly, like a bird.'

She scratched at the blisters on her braces. We all lay there, thinking about it.

'And there's no pain either,' said Pete. 'No one dies or gets ill. If you fall, the ground turns soft and you bounce back up again.'

The room was silent. In the glow of the fire it was as if the house was expanding around us, like it was growing bigger, or we were growing smaller. I smiled.

'I think you get to see your whole life again,' I said. 'You can choose the best part of your life, the moment you were most happy, and you live in it. Forever. And it never stops or gets old or dies or feels any different.'

There was a pause.

'The happiest moment of your life?' said Orlaith, her voice sounding further away now. 'Like what?'

I thought about it.

'In Skirting,' I said, 'Dad used to work late. And some nights – I don't know why, it wasn't always – Mum would let me stay up. I'd make Lego with her, in front of the TV. And then when we heard Dad's car on the drive she'd grab me in her arms and sneak me up to bed and hide me under the duvet, laughing. Because it was our secret. And it felt dangerous, but it was safe at the same time.' I smiled. 'That's where I'd go. That'd never happen now. They're both so – terrified. Of everything.

215

They're like a bomb, ready to go off.'

Callum lay back, his hands behind his head.

'You're all wrong,' he said. 'I reckon when you die, you get to live other lives. You know, better lives than your own. So you get to do things you'd never done before, and be people other than you. Or you could go back to your own life, and try it all over again.'

I looked at him. 'Why?'

Callum sighed. '*Duh* – so if you did stuff wrong the first time, you can get it right the second time! Think about it – if you kept trying something over and over, eventually you'd end up, like, a millionaire.' He smiled. 'But for me, it's no competition. I'd go back and watch Miss Pewlish somersault backwards into that bin – every time.'

We snorted with laughter. Ceri turned to Orlaith.

'What about you, Orlaith?' she said. 'What do you think Heaven is like?'

Orlaith paused. She looked at the ceiling.

'I don't know,' she said, flatly. 'I don't know if anywhere like that even exists.' She sighed. 'But wherever it is, it's got to be better than Barrow – right?'

Orlaith laughed bitterly, pulling at her hair.

'All I ever wanted was to get to the Valley Academy,' she said quietly. 'It was my only way out of there. Out of Barrow. Away from my dad. To go to university – to be like my mum.' She fell silent. 'And now, I've screwed it all up. Being here, in this house – it's probably the furthest I'll ever get in my life. This is the best it's ever going to be.'

We stared at the ceiling. It danced with light, wrapping around us, casting our shadows across the walls like monuments.

'I don't know,' I said. 'I think this is quite nice.'

No one spoke. I lay back, thinking of my grandparents, and my mum and my dad. I thought about the others, and their parents too. I wondered who had lived in this house before, and what they'd been like, and if they ever could have guessed what would happen inside this room after they were long gone.

'Do you think we'll make it?' said a voice.

I don't know who asked it. I was falling asleep, and I wasn't really listening any more. I was lost to the sounds of the house, to the wind and the rain and the crackle of dying embers in the fire. I gazed at the ceiling and the walls. The room grew and grew around us, like a balloon that could never burst.

20

The North Caves

Orlaith stood ahead of us, staring up at the jet-black storm clouds in the distance.

'No,' she whispered.

The North Caves loomed before us. They were hundreds of feet high for miles in either direction, a vertical white wall of raw gouges and crumbling scars that cut through the valley like it had simply fallen from the sky long ago.

There was no tornado in sight.

I looked to the sky above the Caves. The storm clouds lay far in the distance, throwing the shadow of the mountain onto us and casting us into darkness. Orlaith shook her head.

'It . . . it can't have done,' she begged. 'It's not possible. It . . . it *can't* have . . .'

I didn't dare to look at the others. Instead, I kept my eyes fixed on the back of Orlaith's head as she lifted the stormtrap to her face, the certainty of what had happened slowly rising up inside me.

'I . . . I thought the traps would be *this* side,' said Orlaith. 'I never thought that . . .'

She turned to face us, her shoulders swamped in the enormous jacket that hung down over her arms, and I finally saw the look in her eyes. I turned to the others, and sure enough, in every face I saw the same expression, the look of disbelief slowly stained by the terrible understanding of what had happened.

The tornado should have been right in front of us. But it wasn't. We had misread the map. The stormtraps lay on the other side of the North Caves. There was no way we could possibly get to them now.

'You're . . . you're joking, aren't you?'

Callum stepped forwards, his eyes wide and confused.

'I mean, it doesn't matter if the tornado's over there,' he said. 'We can – we can still get to it, right?'

We looked at the enormous cliff wall ahead. It looked hopeless. I stared at the dead earth around me. Where we stood was supposed to be the heartland of all the bears in the valleys. But it was hard to imagine *anything* could live out here, in a place like this. The whole landscape was white as death. There was not a plant, not a tree, not a blade of grass in sight.

And there it was again – the question that had been on my mind all last night, and all this morning. Something that had been buried deep down inside me, since the first day my parents told me about the bears.

I looked to the darkness of the Caves. It was time to find out the answer for myself.

I marched straight up to a hole that lay in the cliff face ahead of us. The others jumped back in shock.

'Owen, careful!' Ceri shouted.

I ignored her, and stood before the cave entrance. It gaped like a jagged open mouth before me, groaning with the weight of the wind drawn through it, roaring as if in pain or hunger, swallowing everything into the darkness. I turned to the others.

'We can still make it,' I said, 'if we go through the mountain. And out the other side. Right now, while we still have time.'

The others stood, rooted to the spot.

'Owen,' said Ceri, 'we can't go in *there* . . .'

'Why not?' I said suddenly, cutting her off. 'We've done everything else they told us we couldn't do, haven't we? Why not this?'

The wind howled out of the Caves behind me. I breathed it in, filling my lungs with the power of it.

'They keep us frightened,' I said. 'They tell us we can't do anything. And we've *listened* to them.' I pointed a finger behind them. 'Well, you saw those people in Skirting – they didn't look frightened to me. They were getting on with their lives.' I held out my hands angrily. 'Why can't we be like that? What's the alternative – be like Miss Pewlish? Or like our parents? Frightened until we die?'

The others looked at me, their faces unreadable.

'Not me,' I said. 'Not any more. I'm sick of being afraid.' I turned to face the cave entrance. 'I'm going to find out what everyone's so frightened of.'

The mouth of the cave roared in front of me, fluttering the baggy suit at my shoulders, sucking me in. I stepped forwards.

'He . . . he's insane!' came Callum's voice from behind me. 'We can't let him go in there! The bears'll come for us once they're done with him! We have to . . .'

Callum trailed off. I suddenly felt a warm hand take mine, wrapping entirely around it. I looked up. Pete stood alongside me. Next to him was Ceri. Orlaith appeared beside them, her hair whipping to a frenzy in the breeze.

'You're not going in there on your own,' she said.

We smiled, and together we walked towards the mouth of the Caves. There was not a single shaft of sunlight beyond its jagged mouth. It sucked in the valley air hungrily, moaning and moaning, a low and constant warning.

'You idiots!' came Callum's voice. 'Don't go in there! You – you'll die!'

We stepped inside the Caves. The cold and the damp closed around us, and the sunlight went out as if it had never been there at all.

And suddenly I felt another hand grab mine in the dark, furtive and desperate. I didn't startle. I knew exactly who it was.

'Please,' came Callum's voice at my ear. 'Don't leave me out there.'

I squeezed his hand, and together the Tornado Chasers made their way into the darkness.

It was a different world inside. The wind blasted against us one moment and sucked us in the next, a freezing tide that carried with it the scent of deepest, oldest stone. The rocks were clammy underfoot, and the sides jagged, the ceiling wet and dripping. We crept on, step by step, our ears pricked and heartbeats thumping. Soon we felt the sides fall away entirely, and we were walled only in darkness.

There was a sudden *click* beside me, and a red light flashed on. Orlaith held the stormtrap high above her. The light blinked on and off, casting the Caves around us in a dull red glow. We were standing in the centre of a great cavern, the roof clustered with ancient stalactites, the walls knotted with twisting white ropes of water. Along the walls lay dozens of stone passageways, tunnelling sideways and downwards and all different directions into the mountain. There was no way of knowing which one was right.

'Everyone, listen,' came Orlaith's voice beside me. 'Listen to the wind. Wherever it's coming from, that's the way out.'

We clenched hands, and listened. The wind bellowed all around us like it came from every direction. It echoed and thrummed on the walls as it was sucked through the cavern, a single reverberating low note. We listened past our own breathing, fast and frightened. We listened past the hammering of our heartbeats in our chests, in our necks, everywhere. The red blinked on and off, on and off.

And then, I heard it.

'That one,' I cried. 'It's coming from that one! There!'

I pointed down a tunnel on the far wall. The inside

trembled and echoed like the throat of a great monster, and at the very end we could see it now – a trickle of light from outside. I grabbed the other's hands and ran forwards.

'Let's get out of here, quick!' I said. 'Before . . .'

Scrape.

I whipped my head round.

'What was that?'

A movement. A scuff on rock. I squeezed the hands either side of me. They squeezed back – they had heard it too. We stood, heads held high, eyes open, ears searching. The Caves held still. Water trickled down ancient rocks. The wind howled.

Scrape.

Ceri thrust out a hand. 'From down there! That tunnel! It . . .'

She trailed off, and the skin of her palm immediately turned ice-cold in my grip. I looked down the tunnel, and my stomach heaved.

It was the tunnel we had just come from.

Scrape.

Something was coming after us.

'It's . . . it's the bears!' cried Callum, shaking from head to foot. 'They've found us!'

I didn't even think – I took their hands and charged

blindly across the cavern, towards the tunnel of faint light that lay on the other side.

'*Down here!*' I cried. '*Quick!*'

We flung ourselves into the tunnel and wound away from the darkness, running against the wind, the stormtrap flashing the tunnel red and black around us. Our feet stumbled and snagged on the slimy floor, and our fingers scrabbled feebly against the wet and jagged rocks.

'*It's behind us!*' cried Ceri. '*Owen, I can hear it, it's catching up . . .*'

And then all of a sudden there it was – the shaft of light, ahead of us, spilling around the end of the tunnel. The way out.

'Keep going!' I cried. 'It's right here, the exit's right . . .'

I charged around the corner and stopped. The tunnel ended right there, dead. There was nothing but a stone wall.

I looked up, and my blood ran cold. Far above us, a hundred feet at least, lay a hole in the ceiling. The wind roared and howled down the stone tower that led to it, the single note it struck now even more hollow and helpless than before. It was the only way out. And there was no way we could ever reach it.

Orlaith flew out of the darkness behind me, and then

Callum, the look on his face one of pure, open fear. He scrambled at the rock walls hopelessly.

'*Oh God no, please!*' he begged. '*Please, not the bears, please!*'

Pete charged out after him, his eyes wide and full of terror, Ceri slung over his shoulder.

'*It's right behind us!*' she screamed.

Scrape.

The sound was close – closer than any of us could have guessed. We threw ourselves to the stone wall and pressed up against it. There was nothing we could do now – nowhere left to run. It was right behind us. We looked at each other.

'Don't be afraid of it!' I cried.

I took their hands, and gripped them tight.

'*Don't let it know you're frightened!*'

The tunnel ahead was still. The wind whined above us, growing and dying. We waited in silence, our hands clenched. And then, from the darkness ahead, came a single voice.

'That's enough now, children.'

A light flashed on – a torch, held below the face of a man. For a moment, it was impossible to see who it was. All we saw were the black orbs of his glasses, and the pale head that floated alone in the air like a ghost. And then he stepped forwards, and the black suit became clear, and the man emerged fully into the light.

The Warden switched off the torch, and looked at us. 'Time to go home,' he said.

21

The Truth

The wind groaned down the stone drop against us, louder now, keener, trembling the stones. The tornado outside was creeping closer. The Warden stood and stared at us, taking each of us into his black gaze, one by one. His eyes stopped on Pete.

'Put her down,' he said, his voice a blank.

Pete carefully lowered Ceri to the ground. The Warden looked at us. He was tall and pale, a shop-front mannequin.

And then suddenly his face changed. He stood up straight, and his jaw clenched.

'Do you have *any* idea how much you've frightened everyone?'

His voice was furious. The wind howled down against us.

'I've got two County officers outside, combing the valley for you,' said the Warden. 'They're both standing within a few hundred feet of a tornado right now – because of you.'

He faced us, half cast in shadow. I looked at the man I had been taught to be frightened of. Behind the dark orbs of his eyes it was impossible to see what he was looking at, or what he saw when he looked at us. All I could see was myself, reflected back in his glasses. I looked so much smaller than him.

'We're getting out of here now,' said the Warden. 'Before . . .'

'Before what?' I said suddenly, cutting him off.

The Warden looked at me, taken aback. I stepped forwards, and stared into his glasses. It was strange to see myself without my helmet. My eyes unafraid.

'Before the bears get us, you mean?'

We faced each other. The Warden stayed looking at me, his face saying nothing.

'Yes,' he said after a pause. 'Yes, exactly. Before the bears . . .'

'We left Barrow three days ago,' I said, cutting him off again. 'Do you know how many bears we've seen in that time? *None.* No tracks. No fur. No sounds . . . nothing.' I stared at him. 'I lived in Skirting for *ten years* without once seeing one. Without even hearing anyone talk about them.' I glared at him. 'How is that possible?'

The Warden held still, his gaze resting on me, as if deciding what to do.

'So what's the truth?'

The Warden stepped back a pace. He took us in.

'Alright,' he said. 'You win. There are no bears in the valleys.'

The others stared at him in shocked silence. Callum stepped forwards, his head shaking.

'B-but . . . there *must* be,' he stuttered. 'When the tornado hit the bear sanctuary in High Folly, they . . .'

'There is no village called High Folly,' said the Warden. 'No bear sanctuary either. They were all made up. Just a story.'

Orlaith stepped forwards, looking him in the eye.

'You lied to us?' she asked.

The Warden waited for a moment, thinking this over. Then, very slowly, he nodded.

'Yes,' he said. 'We did.'

He fell silent. The wind roared above us again, and the tunnel walls trembled. The tornado was getting closer. Ceri suddenly flew forwards.

'Well, you won't get away with this!' she cried. 'Not any more! If you think I'm going to let my little sister grow up like that, thinking there's something out there to be afraid of . . .' She punched the air triumphantly. 'When we get back to Barrow, I'm telling everyone! The parents, the press, the teachers . . . everyone! They'll all know about what you've said, before . . .'

'Ceri.'

Ceri stopped. Orlaith had put a hand on her shoulder.

'They already know,' she said quietly. 'They're all in on it.'

Ceri stood for a moment, stupefied. Her eyes widened.

'But . . . but my parents . . .'

'All of them,' Orlaith repeated.

The tunnel filled with another freezing bite of air. The Warden folded his hands.

'Barrow was built for parents who want to protect their children,' he said. 'After the last tornado hit, a lot of people felt none of the villages were safe any more. Even though the stormtraps could keep tornadoes at a safe distance from any village, people were convinced they weren't enough. So they decided to make a village that was completely secure. A place where no child would ever risk getting into accidents, or misbehaving, or going missing. Where they were kept indoors

231

with curfews and Storm Laws. Where they were too frightened to ever risk their lives.'

He stepped towards us again. We shrank back to the wall.

'And to stop them from leaving the village, they started telling stories. About bears in the valleys that ate children. That stalked the streets each night. Finding those who disobeyed the laws. Punishing those who were curious.'

'And the County Detention Centre,' said Orlaith bitterly. 'That helps keep everyone in line, does it?'

The Warden thought about it, and nodded.

'Most children, yes. Those who work out the truth, though . . . well, we send them lots of different places. Villages outside of the valleys. Anywhere but Barrow.' He sighed. 'As for the five of you . . .'

Orlaith suddenly ran forwards and shoved him, hard. The Warden looked at her in shock. Her eyes were furious.

'You coward!' she spat. 'You know about all this, and you do nothing about it? *How can you . . .*'

The Warden didn't even pause.

'Because I know what it's like to lose someone you love,' he said.

The wind suddenly blew up our backs, heaving back

up through the tunnel. The Warden loomed over us.

'You wanted the truth,' he said, 'and I gave it to you. And now – it's over. Your adventure is done. I'm taking you to the County Detention Centre, and I'm doing it before *that* – ' He pointed up the stone tunnel, where the tornado roared and bellowed against us – 'gets any closer!'

He reached out to us.

'Take my hand,' he said.

Not one of us took it. I looked at it, hovering alone in the air before us. I thought of all the times I'd been told to take an adult's hand. Because they knew what they were doing. Because they'd keep us safe. Because they wanted to help us. I never once thought that I'd ever have to question what adults told me.

I looked up at the Warden, at my face reflecting in his glasses.

'No,' I said. 'We're not coming with you.'

The Warden's mouth flickered for a moment. He did not move his hand.

'I'm going to explain this one more time,' he said. 'And I'm going to explain it very carefully, so that you understand exactly what I'm saying.'

He reached into his suit. With the careful and deliberate movement of a hunter he drew out a black

233

baton and held it out in front of him. It was made of hard metal, and glinted in the light.

'Take my hand,' he repeated.

The wind shrieked down the tunnel, and this time it was so strong that the very clothes on our bodies trembled, and for a moment the glasses seemed to lift from the Warden's face. It was as if the power of the tornado itself was somehow filling us from the ground up, entering our blood and trying to take us to somewhere or something undiscovered. I looked up at, at the man behind the glasses, and I saw his eyes were frightened.

The five of us held hands, and stood in front of him.

'We're not coming with you,' I repeated.

The Warden looked at us in shock. Then he took a step back, and raised the baton above his head.

'Have it your way,' he said.

And with a sudden great howl of wind the baton was plucked straight out of the Warden's hand.

We gasped. All six of us watched the baton shoot up the stone tower, clattering against the jagged rocks. Our mouths fell open.

'What the . . .' the Warden managed.

And then he couldn't say anything any more, because the wind in the tunnel screamed so loud our ears rang, and the air was drawn straight out of our chests as if by force, and with a great lurch each and every one of us was thrust spiralling up through the stone tunnel.

The floor disappeared below us. We tumbled up, clutching each other's hands and shrieking in amazement. The Warden scrambled hopelessly in the air below us, trying to grab hold of something. The baton bounced against the walls above us, flying towards the opening in the roof like it was little more than a twig.

'W-what's happening?' I gasped.

'It's the tornado!' Orlaith laughed, pinwheeling beside me. 'The wind in the valley outside . . . it's sucking us straight up the tunnel! We're going to make it . . .'

'*No!*' came the Warden's voice from beneath us. '*I'm not letting you go!*'

With a great lunge the Warden heaved through the air and clamped his hand around Pete's leg. He started heaving the five of us down.

'Oh no!' Ceri cried. 'We're going to fall!'

She was right. With the Warden hanging on to us we were too heavy, and our climb had slowed. I looked down in terror. The drop back to the stone floor was a long way down.

'Stop!' I begged. 'You have to let go or you'll kill us all . . . !'

Slowly, bit by bit, the clutch of wind in the tunnel dropped. Soon, it would break completely. The walls came to a stop beside us. The Warden grit his teeth.

'*I'm – not – letting – you – go!*' he cried.

CLANG.

There was a sharp noise above us, and then another, and another. We looked up just as the Warden's baton spun lethally back down the tunnel towards us. It missed Pete by a hair's breadth, and with a sickening CRACK struck the Warden right on top of his head. He gave a short cry of pain, and immediately let go of Pete's ankle, plummeting to the floor below.

The second he did the wind bellowed through the stone tunnel again, we lurched back up. The stones around us trembled with the strength of the tornado. Orlaith clutched onto us tightly.

'*This is it!*' Orlaith screamed. '*We're going through the roof! Hold on!*'

Our ears popped, and our heads buzzed, and our hearts felt like roaring engines inside of us, and together we were flung up, up past the jagged rocks that stuck out at all angles and tumbled through the hole in the ceiling, screaming and laughing in disbelief. And then we were flying through the valley outside, the wind freezing and powerful and somehow coming at us in all directions,

236

flinging us back down to earth . . .

I crashed down onto the grass of a hillside, sprawling into rocks and tumbling down the slope until I came to a stop. My whole body sang to me.

'*Owen!*'

I pushed myself up from the ground. Behind me, the others had clambered to their feet and stood facing the horizon in a line. Their hair and clothes whipped around them, and their mouths hung open. I turned around.

The tornado before us filled the width of the valley. Above it lay jet-black clouds, shot through with veins of deepest red like a sky made of burning coals. Around it in every direction lay a spiral of trees, cars, bricks, animals, tankers, rocks, statues, chimneys and barbed wire that had caught in the vortex, spinning and spinning and crashing against the valley's sides, shredding them to dust. But at the centre of it all, like a shape in the fog of a glass, was a spiralling white core of pure wind, goring through the earth, a wall of destruction that headed straight for us.

We were being dragged towards it, our feet slipping and stumbling along the grass. The wind was unbelievable, the sheer power of it tearing at the skin on our faces. And it was growing. I turned to the others.

'*This is it!*' I screamed. '*Do we still do it?*'

'*Are you kidding?*' Orlaith cried out. '*We can't go back now, Owen!*'

I shook my head. '*I mean . . .*'

'I know *what you mean*,' she shouted. She fixed me with one of her looks. '*But this is about more than taking a picture now. And I'm saying: we can't go back.*'

I looked at her in shock. She kept her gaze fixed on me, without blinking, her face terrified and delighted all at once. She really meant it. The tornado bellowed through the valley towards us, the ground either side pelted with car doors and garden gates that smashed into the ground beside us and missed us by inches. I turned to the others. They looked frightened too. *I* was frightened. I don't think I had ever been more frightened in my life.

But I had never felt so alive.

'*All of us?*' I said.

Ceri and Pete nodded, their breaths short, their eyes wide and their faces flushed. They understood. Only Callum stayed still, staring at the distance.

' . . . *Callum?*' I said.

His eyes were fixed onto the tornado that roared towards us. He was breathing in and out, in and out, and he was trembling. I had never seen him so frightened. I reached out and took his shoulder.

'*Callum.*'

His eyes shot back to me, desperate, terrified.

'*You don't have to come with us,*' I said. '*We won't make you. You're one of us. You can go if you want to.*'

He looked back at me, his chest heaving, his eyes torn. Then, he swallowed, and shook himself.

'*No!*' he cried. '*I came here to chase a tornado, and I'm going to do it!*'

He took our hands, and held them up to the storm.

'*Because we,*' he shouted, '*are Tornado Chasers!*'

'*And we are not afraid!*' we all screamed with him.

At that moment the wind bellowed against us, and we were flattened straight onto the ground. I tried to cling onto the grass but it gave way in my hands, the soil scattering and soaring through the air towards the storm. We were being dragged towards it.

'*I can't hold on!*' I cried.

A hand grabbed mine. I looked up. Pete was clutching a rock that lay at the cave entrance, and was holding onto Ceri. Orlaith held onto one of Ceri's leg braces with one hand and Callum with the other, who held onto me.

And then I realised that I was being lifted straight off the ground, and so were the others, trailing in a line from Pete like a kite in the wind. The world seemed to turn upside down, and the force of it crushed us from all sides, spinning us around and around and pressing against us. Thunder and lightning exploded above us. It was like the world was breaking apart.

'Ceri!' Orlaith screamed. 'The photo! Now!'

Ceri's camera hovered in the air before her, attached to her by the strap round her neck. She reached out for it frantically with her free hand, and with a cry of effort dragged it towards her. The tornado howled into black around us, and there seemed to be nothing else in the world but loudness and pain and confusion.

Ceri turned the camera towards us and took a picture.

And with that, the tornado began to pass.

The wind began to drop. The roar subsided, bit by bit. The air began to lift into lightness again. The crushing around us disappeared, and we began to lower to the ground.

One by one we let go of each other, and dropped onto the grass. We lay dazed for a moment, before picking ourselves up and looking around. The valley was devastated. Everywhere we looked were the fallen remains of the storm. The ground itself had been stripped bare, as if by acid.

But we had survived. The Tornado Chasers had done

it. We had fought against the impossible, and we had won. I leapt to my feet.

'*We did it!*' I cried. '*We did it, we did it!*'

In the distance the tornado roared away, pushed by the last of the stormtraps into the North. We clutched each other.

'*We did it!*' we cried.

And together we danced along the sides of the valley, our arms around each other, as far away the—

No.

241

'*Because we,*' he shouted, '*are Tornado Chasers!*'

'*And we are not afra—!*'

Our words were cut off by an almighty crash beside us. We swung round, and gasped. The tornado was even closer now, bellowing down the valley towards us. And there, not a hundred feet away, an enormous black van had dropped out of the sky, bashed and battered by days inside the storm. It had hit the ground, and was tumbling towards us at lightning speed. I cried in fear.

'*It's going to hit us!*' I shouted.

Callum leapt into action.

'*Quick!*' he said. '*When I say jump, everybody jumps! Get it?*'

Orlaith grabbed him. '*Are you crazy?*'

'*Just do it!*' he ordered.

The van still tumbled towards us, its doors ripped open, its windscreen shattered.

'*Ready?*' said Callum. '*One, two . . . jump!*'

Everyone jumped, and in that exact second we flew inside the van and hit the back wall with a tremendous THUMP, knocking the air out of ourselves. I glanced up. The van had bounced hard on the ground and was now airborne again, spiralling through the air as the tornado's strength swung it round and round the valley.

'Ceri, *quick!*' cried Callum, springing back into action. '*The photo!*'

Ceri sat up, dazed, and fumbled for the camera slung around her neck. Callum grabbed the rest of us.

'*Everyone stand by the back doors!*' he ordered. '*We don't have much time before the van hits the ground again!*'

The doors of the van had been ripped off long ago. On unsteady feet the four of us stood by the gaping hole as the van soared like a jet plane through the air, the tornado now a solid wall of wind behind us.

'*Now, Ceri!*' Callum screamed. '*It's our only chance!*'

At once Ceri took the photo. Without a second to spare Callum grabbed us and swung us round to the open doors. I gasped in amazement. The van was plummeting back to the earth again, the ground flying towards us.

'*JUMP!*' Callum cried.

The five of us flew screaming out of the van just as it hit the ground with another sickening *CRASH*, shattering into scrap on the rocks beneath us. One by one we sprawled across the ground and looked up, dazed. In the distance the tornado had moved on, on towards the North.

Orlaith turned to Callum with a smile.

'Callum – you did it!' she cried. 'You actually did it!'

I laughed. 'Callum, you're a hero!'

Callum smiled, and put his arms around us.

'Oh, it was nothing, 'he said. 'Anything for my friends.'

We ran to him, hugging each other and laughing and laughing as—

No.

'*Because we,*' he shouted, '*are Tornado Chasers!*'

'*And we are not afraid!*' we all screamed with him.

The five of us held hands, and turned to face the tornado. It bellowed towards us down the valley, obliterating everything in its path, destroying all, leaving nothing.

'Owen.'

I turned around. Callum was looking at me.

'Before we do this,' he said. 'I need to talk to you.'

I balked. 'Callum, we can't talk now . . .'

'No,' he said. 'I mean it! I have to talk to you because I might not ever get the chance again!'

The tornado whipped around us, howling, howling. Callum stared at me, trying to find the right words.

'I'm sorry I was so horrible to you,' he shouted over the wind. 'All those times I told you you were pathetic and laughed at you, I'm really really sorry. I wish I'd never even said it. There are so many things I did that I wish I hadn't done. ~~You were~~ You're the bravest one out of all of us. That's why I was always so horrible to you. I ~~thought~~ knew I could never be like you.'

The wind raged towards us, ~~erasin~~ destroying everything in the valley.

'And I'm sorry for those times I pushed you in the nettles,' he said. '~~I did it because~~ I'm just sorry. I'm just so sorry.'

The tornado fell on us and devoured us, and ~~Owen~~ I reached out my hand.

'Callum,' I said. 'It's OK. I forgive you.'

~~He~~

I

I wrote plenty more endings like those. I wrote hundreds. And they all went straight out the window. Because, Warden, I don't know what happened to the others after Owen told me that I could leave. I don't know because I took his offer. I ran away. I never saw the tornado.

This is why they call me Callum the Coward.

I kept running until the County officers found me in the next valley, and arrested me, and locked me in the back of their van while they went and searched for the others. They didn't find them, of course - as well you know, Warden. There wasn't a trace left of them. They combed the valleys for five days. And when they found nothing, all eyes turned to me.

247

They asked me endless questions about what had happened. Why hadn't I disappeared with my friends? Why had we done it? Where had Owen gone? What happened to Ceri? To Pete? To Orlaith? Why are you the only one left, Callum? What makes you so special?

What happened to them, Callum?

I said nothing. I couldn't bring myself to tell them the simple truth: that the others had been brave enough to stay, and I hadn't. And then after a while, whenever I did start talking, the sound of my own voice made me feel sick. I had always talked to get myself out of everything, to lie, or bully, or cheat. Now, I didn't want to talk any more. I didn't trust anything that I had to say.

Neither did my parents. They came back home for a bit to see me - for a bit. They told me that I had to tell the police everything. And then they signed the papers for my internment, and left. My babysitter drove me to County herself. She put me in my cell, kissed my head, and left. And with that, I had lost everything.

That is how I began my time as an inmate of the County Detention Centre. That is where I sat in my empty cell, scared and sad, and the guards told me that I had better start talking. Because until I did, and I finally told everyone what had happened, then I would never leave.

And here it is. My story. You've finally found it, Warden. Well done!

I wonder what you thought when you started reading it. I wonder if you had any idea why I decided to write my story as Owen. Why didn't I write it as myself - as Callum the bully, the liar, the coward, the deserter?

Is it really such a mystery to you?

No one wants to read about someone who ran away. They want to read about heroes. About people who find the courage when they need it. And I never found mine. I never had any in the first place.

And speaking of running away – there's another mystery here, if I'm not mistaken . . .

Where have I gone?

Well, that's another story entirely.

Which unfortunately I've had to hide somewhere else. Everything will make sense once you find it, promise.

If you find it.

~~Good luck!~~

Yours sincerely,

'Inmate 409?'

As long as I can remember, I've always wanted to be somebody else. Even before I heard of the Tornado Chasers. I never could stand being Callum.

'*Inmate 409?*'

Luckily for me, your name is one of the first things they stop using when you come to County.

I whip round, quickly scrunching up the sheet of paper on the desk before me. I was so busy writing a new ending – where I save Owen and the others by riding away on motorcycles – that I didn't even notice I was being watched. I slip the ball of paper out the window before the guard sees it and turn to the door.

My cell is small and cold. There's not much to look at – a light bulb, a desk, a bed, a sink with a loose tile at the back. The guard is glaring at me through the hatch in the locked door.

'Finally writing your confession, are you?' he snaps.

I say nothing. The guard frowns.

'Oh God,' he groans. 'You're still not talking, are you?'

I nod.

'Big surprise,' he mutters. 'Well, you'd better *start* talking, fast. It's the day of your meeting.'

My heart stops. I knew that this meeting would happen one day. But I didn't know it would be today. The guard unlocks the door.

'Who would have thought,' he said. 'Six months you've had to write that flipping confession, and how much have you done? Not a word!' He laughs. 'You must *love* being here.'

The guard's wrong. I don't love being here. But then, he's wrong about a lot of things. He doesn't know that I have been secretly writing my story this whole time. That it's hidden, page by page, behind the loose tile above the sink. But I don't correct him. I don't want to talk to him, or anyone. I just want to be left alone, and to write my story. That's all I want any more.

'Come on,' says the guard. 'The Warden's waiting.'

He marches me up endless flights of stairs, to the glass door that lies at the end of a long corridor on the very top floor. As it gets closer the surface of my hands starts to prickle, and I feel like I'm about to be sick. We stop outside the door. I look down at the nametag on the wood panel.

THE WARDEN.

It will be the first time I've seen him since the Caves. I try to slow my heartbeat, to calm my breathing, to tell myself that I am not afraid. I can't let him see me be afraid.

'Come in,' says a voice from inside.

I open the door, and I immediately stop. The view

252

– you can see the whole of the valleys here, running in great waves over Barrow and the hills beyond. It's beautiful. This must be the only room in County that doesn't have bars in the glass.

'Well,' says a voice. 'Inmate 409.'

I turn. The Warden sits behind his desk, a paper folder in his hands. He wears his black suit and black glasses. He looks exactly the same as he did that day in the cave, a lifetime ago. The only difference now is the scar across the top of his head, where he must have hit the stone floor. He looks me up and down and raises an eyebrow.

'You thought I was dead, didn't you?' he says dryly. 'Well, I'm sorry to disappoint you. I did *wish* I was dead for a while, seeing as I broke both my legs when I landed, but eventually the County officers found me. Nothing a few months in hospital couldn't solve.'

We stare at each other for a while. At least, I think we do. It's hard to tell what he's looking at behind his glasses. I keep my face blank, my eyes dead. I can't let him see I'm frightened. The Warden waits for me to say something, in vain. After a while he holds out a hand to a wooden chair on the other side of the desk.

'Sit down.'

I sit. The Warden holds up the paper folder and leafs through it. It has a picture of my face on the front, taken back on the first day I was interred. I look much younger.

'Inmate 409,' the Warden reads, his eyes scanning over the file. 'The Tornado Chaser.'

The memory of what happened rises up when he says the words, sudden and unexpected. I have a well of memories inside me, of everything that happened, a deep well that goes down beyond where I can get to them. Most of the time I can ignore it, pretend it's not there, but I feel it now as it rises up, urgent and angry. I breathe gently, and push it back down. The Warden closes the folder and looks at me.

'Do you remember the conditions of your arrest, 409?' he asks.

I nod calmly, but say nothing. The Warden pauses for another moment, and then speaks.

'We said that you had to explain to us exactly what happened. And until you did, we wouldn't be able to let you go.' He folds his arms. 'There are people who need to know how you did it, 409 – so they can prevent anything like that from ever happening again. You do understand, don't you?'

I nod. I understand completely. That is why I cannot tell them anything. If I did tell them what happened, it would all be over. They would release me from County and I'd have to go back home. Back to everyone who knew me.

'So why won't you talk?' asks the Warden.

And for the rest of my life, I'd have to face what happened that day.

I just shrug. The Warden looks at me for a long time.

'You know I used to have children myself, 409?'

I say nothing. The Warden looks at me. I can see myself reflected back in his glasses. I look very small, and very far away.

'It was a long time ago,' he says. He looks me up and down. 'I suppose they'd be about your age by now.'

He pauses for a moment, waiting for a response from me.

'I took the Warden job after they died. I promised myself I would never let any children come to any harm, ever again. That I would dedicate my life to protecting them. So I know what it's like to cope with losing a child. That's how the parents of your friends feel right now, 409. Don't *they* deserve to know what happened?'

I glare at the man sat in front of me. It is a cruel trick for him to play. He leans forward.

'Don't they?'

I nod. Of course they do. I hate him right then, more than anything.

Leave me alone, I scream at him inside my head. *Get away from me. You liar.*

'Then why won't you tell us what happened?'

I look out the window again. It's just past midday, and the sun is beating off the ripples of the valley and making the grass and treetops shine, turning the whole world green. I guess he keeps the window here for a reason.

'I need you to answer me, 409.'

I lick my lips, and clear my throat.

'I . . . I don't know how,' I say weakly.

My voice comes out hoarse and cracked. It's become barely a whisper over the last year. This is because I never speak. When I have to, my voice doesn't even sound like mine any more. It's good. I like it that way.

The Warden looks at his folder again.

'It says here you were told you could write it down,' said the Warden. 'Only the guard here tells me you haven't written anything in six months. Is that true?'

I hide my eyes and quickly nod. It is a lie, of course. But no one knows that. I can't ever let them know. The Warden eyes me critically.

'It's almost like you don't want to leave,' he says quietly.

He keeps his gaze fixed on me, his face expressionless.

The idea suddenly occurs to me that the Warden can see through me, that he can see the truth, that he already knows what happened, what a coward I've been. I stare back at him, trying to make myself a blank page he cannot read.

The Warden waits for me to talk. I say nothing. He sighs, and adjusts himself on his chair.

'I think we need to try another approach,' he says.

He nods to the guard behind me. I hear him walk across the room, and unlock the door, and leave. It is now just me and the Warden. I sit, gazing calmly forward, but my heart is spasming in my chest. I keep my face empty. I can't let him see that I'm frightened.

The Warden stands up. He walks around the desk to the other side, and stands beside me. He looks down at me. I am trying to stop myself from trembling. All I can think about is him in the Caves, holding the baton over our heads. He's as close to me now as he was then. He leans over, even closer.

'Callum,' he says, 'we need to talk about what happened in the Caves.'

And that's too much. My name, the memory of it, and now him right there beside me, just like that day. I suddenly leap to my feet, throwing the chair back behind me.

'*You . . . you liar!*' I cry.

My voice is there, right in front of me, my old voice. I've learned to hide it over the last few months but I can't hide it now. The Warden looks at me in shock.

'Callum, I don't . . .'

'I stayed behind in school for a year!' I spit. 'A *whole year*. And you know why?' I stare at him. 'Go on, you know everything else, don't you?'

I have to look at the reflection in his glasses, at myself as I shout. It makes me even angrier. I clench my teeth.

'*Bears*,' I shout. '*Bears!* All those *stupid* stories about *bears!* Once I left Miss Pewlish's class and went up a year, I wasn't going to get a Home-Time Partner any more, was I? And you know what *that* means? Walking home on your own. I couldn't do it! Everyone thought it was because I was stupid, but I wasn't stupid. *I wasn't stupid!*'

My face burns with the humiliation of it. I clench my fists and grit my teeth and try to drive it down again, the anger and the fear and the sadness inside me, but it's no good. I can't now.

'All those stories about children being eaten . . . I really believed them! So I made sure I'd always have a Home-Time Partner, didn't I? Because I couldn't be left on my own. I tried to hide it but I couldn't. I was . . . I was *frightened!*'

I turn to him. He stands, his face blank.

'That's why we did it!' I cry. 'The whole thing! Leaving the village, chasing the tornado . . . the whole point was to prove that we weren't afraid – but there wasn't even anything to be afraid of! It was all lies!' I shove him. 'Go on, then, talk! It's your turn! *What could you possibly have to say to me that you haven't already said?*'

I fall silent. The Warden stares at me.

'I wanted to apologise to you,' he says. 'I wanted to tell you that . . . that I'm sorry.'

The Warden swallows.

'For everything I said to you that day,' he explains. 'To you and your friends. And the fact I tried to . . . I made a mistake. I didn't do it right. I regret it, hugely. If I *had* done better, I don't know, maybe . . . maybe things would have been different. Maybe your friends would still be here.' He pauses. 'I'm so sorry.'

He finishes. We wait in silence and look at each other. Something has changed, in the space of a few sentences. We're more equal. Maybe it's the light in the office, or my memory, but I notice that the Warden does look different now. From this close, I can see that his hair has grown out a little over the last year. He is, in fact, slightly balding. Maybe that's why he shaves his head. He looks at me, straight on.

'You need to explain what happened, Callum,' he says. 'If you don't, you'll be here for the rest of your life.'

I shake my head. 'But I . . . I can't.'

'Why not?'

I clear my throat. It hurts. I haven't spoken this much in a long time.

'I . . . I did try to explain,' I say. 'Back when they first questioned me. I really did. But I – I couldn't stand it. I had to try and explain why I did all these things I did, why I said things . . . and most of the time I didn't even know why myself. I look back at what I did, and I hate myself for it.'

The Warden looks at me. He's confused.

'What do you mean, what you did?'

I shuffle slightly. 'I don't want to talk about it.'

The Warden suddenly steps forward. He looks genuinely concerned.

'Callum – you know you didn't do anything wrong, don't you?'

It's too much. The memories rise up inside me, everything that I've worked so hard not to think about. I push myself backwards.

'I want to go now,' I say.

I push myself backwards but I'm in a corner. There's

nowhere to go. The Warden steps towards me.

'Callum, I'm serious,' he says. 'You didn't do anything wrong. You can't punish yourself like this. Why don't you give yourself a chance and . . .'

'Because I don't want to!' I shout. 'Leave me alone! Let me go!'

The memories are rising up. The Warden doesn't stop.

'Why are you so frightened, Callum?' he says. 'Why can't you tell us what happened, and start over again?'

'*Because I don't deserve it!*'

It's coming out of me now and I'm terrified, I can't stop it. The Warden steps forward.

'Why don't you deserve it, Callum?'

'*Because of what I did!*' I cry, slamming my hands against the wall behind me. I'm trying to stop it coming out but the Warden keeps stepping towards me. He's close to me now. There's nowhere I can go.

'Callum,' he says, slowly, calmly. 'What could you possibly have done that deserves *this*?'

I leap at him, my chest bursting, and out it comes.

'*I left them!*'

The Warden stands, and watches me. I hang my head and hold it in my hands.

'*I left them.* I just left them there. My friends. My first ever friends. You hear me? I made them go it alone. I . . . I didn't even say goodbye!'

The memory arrives. And at once, I see it. The moment in the Caves when I took Owen's hand and he let me. And I think about every single time I pushed him into the nettles.

'They put up with me all that time,' I say, shaking. 'They put up with me. After everything I said to them and everything I did to them. They didn't laugh at me or call me a coward. Like I would have done to them. They . . . they let me go.'

It was that moment, that exact moment when Owen said I could go, that I knew I had never been a Tornado Chaser, not a real one, not like him. Because if I had been one – a true one down in my heart – I would have thanked him, I would have said sorry, I would have told him how much his friendship had meant to me. But I didn't do any of those things.

'They knew the truth,' I say. 'That I couldn't stand up to it, like they could. And they were right. I wasn't a Tornado Chaser. I was just . . . a coward.'

The Warden steps forward again.

'You were not a coward, Callum,' he says. 'You were frightened. And that is not the same thing as being a coward. Everyone is frightened.'

262

I shake my head. 'No they're not. Not like me. Not all the time.'

The Warden shrugs. 'No, not all the time. But you can't *never* be frightened, Callum. That's not bravery. Bravery is knowing how frightened you are of something, and still doing it anyway.'

As he says it, something suddenly clicks in me. I glare at him.

'That's rich, coming from you!' I spit at him. 'Your job is *lying* to children. Scaring them! Getting them to do what you want! How do you think I felt, standing there in the Caves, thinking a bear was coming towards me? I thought I was going to die! And then, when we tried to escape . . . you *attacked us*!'

The room is silent suddenly. This time, the Warden does not move. He looks at me.

'I didn't mean to do it,' he says. 'I wasn't trying to scare you. I didn't want to hurt you. I wasn't even angry.'

'Then why did you do it?' I shout.

He pauses for a moment. And then slowly, he reaches up, and takes off his glasses.

'I did it because I thought that you'd get away from me,' he says. 'Because I thought everything that had happened to me would happen again. Because I thought that I'd fail. That I'd lose you.'

I see his eyes properly for the first time. They are old and green and marked with lines of pain, lines that show what he has been through. They are the kindest and gentlest eyes I have ever seen. And I finally understand why he has to wear glasses.

'Because I was frightened,' he says quietly.

The door suddenly opens behind me, and I spin round. The guard has walked back in.

'Everything OK in here, sir?' he asks.

I turn back to the Warden. His face is blank once more, a shop-front mannequin. He has put his glasses back on. All I can see is myself reflected in them.

But I'm shocked at what I see. I'm different to the boy that walked in. Something has changed. The Warden clears his throat, and for a second I'm certain he's shaking.

'Get 409 as much paper as he wants,' he says. 'He has a lot of writing to do.'

■ ■ ■

The guard closes my cell door behind me.

Scrape.

A stack of paper has been pushed under the doorway behind me. It is quickly followed by a pencil.

I look out the window of my cell. The view from here is not like the one in the Warden's office. The fields outside my window are landfill, stretching right on towards the horizon. The people of Barrow ship their rubbish out here, where they can't see it, and it piles up and surrounds the valley like an ocean. Birds are swooping down from the clouds, picking at it in great shifting flocks, right up the hills.

I push my head against the bars and look down. There, just beneath my window, lies an enormous mound of scrunched-up paper balls. All of them are mine, each one a different ending that I started, and abandoned, and thrown away. I found the paper any way I could – ripped it out of books, stole it from other cells, made my handwriting tiny and cramped and spidery to fit as much possible onto the page. Anything to get more than one sheet a week. There must be hundreds of them down there. There are so many that the wind has formed them into a drift against the wall.

The wind.

I look out over the valley. The sun is beginning to set now, dipping behind the hills. I can see the stormtraps along the valley top, blinking in the dusk. A steady wind is blowing, growing stronger, blowing into my room. It lifts the sheets of paper off the floor beside me, flinging them around the cell like a tornado, taking me to places beyond the mountains.

This notepaper is kindly provided for the inmates of
THE COUNTY DETENTION CENTRE
Use one sheet per week
No scribbling

Dear Warden,

Congratulations! You've finally found my last letter. I knew you would.

You certainly would have had to work hard to look through every single scrunched-up paper ball in the pile outside my cell window. You may find some pages in there about the day of our meeting, and many different endings that I wrote for my story. There are quite a lot of them now. Thousands, in fact. You can do whatever you want with them — I don't have a use for them any more. Choose whichever you think is best.

I'd appreciate it if you kept going through the pile. Somewhere in there, you'll find a letter I have written to the people of Barrow. It's important that it gets to them. It also explains where I've gone to - if you haven't already worked that out for yourself by now. I'm sure you have.

Don't bother sending any search parties after me. It will be too late. I know where I'm going now, and I know why I want to do it. It feels good to say that, and to mean it, for the first time ever. I hope one day you'll know what I mean.

~~Yours s~~

Thank you.

Dear parents and teachers of Barrow,

As I write this I'm standing on the roof of the County Detention Centre, looking out over the valley around me. Despite all the rubbish that you send here, it can look very beautiful. Now is a very good example. A new tornado landed last night. In the distance I can see the flickering stormtraps along the hilltops, and hear their distant warning cry. Right now, you will all be tucked in safely at home, waiting for the storm to pass. But not me.

In a moment, I will scrunch this letter up into a ball and throw it off the roof, just as I have thrown out many other pages before it. It will land with the thousands of others that are piled up beneath my cell window. The pile is pretty high now. There are so many that they will easily cushion my fall when I jump off. From there, it is a simple two-day walk across the valley to the Great North Caves. I know I will get there before the tornado does. And then, I will meet it head-on.

I decided a long time ago that I was going to do this. I decided that I was going to go against everything that I was brought up to believe - that living in fear is better than standing up against what frightens you. It is a lesson that you taught me well, Barrow - one that you still teach your children.

I'm afraid now. I'm afraid of what lies ahead of me, but unlike you I'm not going to let it stop me. The world is a frightening place, and I don't want to run from it any longer. I've run away from a lot of things. I've had enough. I want to see what happens when I stop.

And I want to see my friends again too, more than anything. I want to see where they went.

270

I hope this letter will make you change your minds about what you've done. Perhaps you might abandon Barrow altogether and start showing your children how to live with fear rather than how to hide from it. But I think it's much too late for that now. I don't think you'll even listen.

But your children might.

Yours sincerely,

~~INM~~
CALLUM BRENNER

'Callum?'

His eyes were fixed onto the tornado that roared towards us. He was breathing in and out, in and out, and he was trembling. I had never seen him so frightened. I reached out and took his shoulder.

'Callum.'

His eyes shot back to me, desperate, terrified.

'You don't have to come with us,' I said. 'We won't make

you. You're one of us. You can go if you want to.'

He looked back at me, his chest heaving, his eyes torn. They darted backwards and forwards between me and the tornado. Then he turned and ran, until the grey haze of the rain around us swallowed him completely.

And then there were four of us.

I turned to the others.

'Well,' I said. 'Shall we?'

We took each other's hands. Me, Pete, Ceri and Orlaith, in a line, facing the tornado. We walked slowly, step by step, towards the wall of wind that bore towards us. Trees plummeted around us, splintering into twigs against the rocks. The storm howled. The camera around Ceri's neck ripped free of its strap and flew into the distance. We didn't need it – not where we were going.

We came to the valley floor, and there it was before us. The tornado crushed us down, buckling our legs, driving us to the ground. We looked at each other. I clutched Orlaith's hand, and she clutched mine, and we all faced forwards.

'We are the Tornado Chasers,' we shouted, 'and we are terrified!'

The wind became a frenzy, thrashing and flailing against us, as if it was the one who was afraid and not us. We clutched onto each other and grit our teeth, weighing ourselves down. The tornado pounded, heaved, screamed, *and then it became even worse somehow, the strength of it unbelievable, the pain greater than anything I'd ever experienced, until I couldn't bear it any longer and –*

And then, there was nothing.

It was as if it had all just stopped. There was absolute silence and stillness and warmth, where just before there had been cold.

I opened my eyes, and looked around me. We were sat in the centre of a clearing. A wall of wind surrounded us, a perfect circle. We could see nothing outside of it.

'It's the eye of the storm,' I whispered.

We slowly got to our feet. It was like we were standing in the centre of a clouded glass. The tornado stood frozen around us.

'It means it's not over,' I said. 'It means there's more to come.'

And at that moment the four of us were lifted off our feet. I gasped. We were being carried up, as if by hands. Then we started to spin. Slowly at first, and then faster, turning with the wind in our square of four. We clung to each other and held our breaths. We spun faster and faster, until the blood raged in our heads and we couldn't hold on to each other any more, and still we kept climbing.

The walls of wind fell away beside us. The valleys lay far below. We could see Barrow, and Skirting, and the Caves, and the quarry, and everywhere that we had been to together, twisting and disappearing away from us. It all seemed so small now, so far away. We watched as the tornado trailed to the North and faded out into nothingness below, its path scrawled onto the world like a pencil mark on paper.

'OWEN!'

The clouds parted, and we emerged into glorious sunlight. Four planes were circling us. They were bi-planes, faded and cracked and cast in black and white, a photo come to life. On the wings, emblazoned across a picture of a spiralling tornado, were the initials: T.C.

The planes immediately froze, like an old film stopped mid-frame. They held in the air before us, as easily as if they were suspended on strings. We had stopped moving, too, floating on our fronts like we were underwater. Two people inside the nearest plane leant out to face us.

'We've been waiting for you,' said my grandparents.

They climbed out onto the wings of their planes, and clutched me to their chests. They were completely black and white, their faces faded and bleached with age.

'We're so proud of you,' they said. 'You did so well. All of you.'

The other Tornado Chaser pilots had climbed out onto the wings of their planes to shake hands with Orlaith and Ceri and Pete, congratulating them in clipped accents.

'Superb work!' said one. 'Very impressive to have made it this side of the portal at your age.'

I glanced up. 'Portal? A portal to where?'

My grandparents laughed. My granddad reached out and took my hand.

'Have a look,' he said.

I looked down at the valleys below. The whole map lay before me, the tornado's path still scrawled across the hills and valleys. And then suddenly, the map began to change – hundreds more paths emerged, different ones, winding their way across the valleys in front of me like they were being drawn by a hundred hands at once. Each path was a different tornado from the past, leaving its mark on the valleys like a brushstroke.

'Keep watching, Owen,' said Grandma, holding my head. 'Don't look away.'

The paths kept adding up, piling and piling on top of one another, generation after generation of storms marked out on a single valley. At first it was little more than a scribble on paper, but then I realised that, bit by bit, the lines were adding up to something greater – they were gradually making a picture. Or a word, a sentence maybe, one that kept changing its mind again and again. Or even more than that – a story written and rewritten across the landscape, one that couldn't be read yet, not until it was finished. They were innumerable now, crossing and criss-crossing each other like a mesh of words and half-words, an entire history of storms written on the ground.

And then, the towns and hills and rivers suddenly slipped out of focus in front of me. They split and separated in endless versions of the same landscape, one for each of the different paths the tornado had taken, layered on top of each other like a pad of tracing paper.

'You see?' said Grandma. 'You can see them all now. They're all here.'

I looked at her in confusion. 'I don't understand.'

Granddad nodded, and took my hand. 'Of course you don't. Let's go take a look at Skirting, shall we?'

In an instant we were above the church in the main square. I could see myself down there on the day we passed through, charging around the corner in a wedding dress as the bride and groom emerged from the church doors in the distance. But that wasn't all. Waves upon waves of other people flowed out the church doors beside them – endless brides and endless grooms, troops of parents with young babies in long white christening gowns, mourners by the thousands, fleets of coffins, all passing younger versions of themselves in the streets without knowing or noticing.

'And there's us!' said Granddad excitedly. 'Right there, in the middle!'

I tried to look through the heaving mass of people below me, but I couldn't. It was almost too much to take in at once.

'I . . . I can't see,' I said.

Grandma waved her hands in front of her, and at once the different layers separated and dissolved until there was only one left. It was a summer's day. A young couple was stepping out the church doors to a small crowd of friends and family, cheering and clapping. Grandma held Granddad's arm tight.

'I never get tired of it,' she said.

I looked down. The whole scene played and replayed in front of me, again and again. It felt new every time. It didn't grow old, and it never would.

Granddad waved his arms, and the layers came back immediately, a thousand years of different lives. The different versions flickered in front of us, generations moving and shifting like leaves on water.

'All you have to do,' he said, 'is decide which one you want to go to.'

The pilots suddenly leapt back into their planes and adjusted their goggles, looking at us expectantly.

'But . . .' my eyes flickered between the others. 'Does that mean we can't go together? What if some of us want to home, and some of us don't? What if we don't see each other again?'

Orlaith placed a hand on my shoulder.

'I don't think it works like that, Owen.'

She was already disappearing in front of my eyes. I looked around for the others. I wanted to talk to them, to ask them what they thought, to hear their ideas, but I couldn't. They weren't there any more. At least, I couldn't see them. But I could still feel them. It was like their hands were still in mine, and they were still out there, right beside me, in another layer that I couldn't quite see.

I looked up. The sun was getting closer towards me now, and it warmed me through like happiness, glowing through my hands as I held them against it. I knew that up here there would be no pain, or unhappiness, or fear. There would be nothing that you couldn't fix or take back. Nothing would ever get old or change or die. Everything would be beautiful. And everything would be perfect.

'So,' said my grandparents, 'where do you want to go?'